MEN OF THE
MORNING STAR

By
EDMOND HAMILTON

I0541535

ARMCHAIR FICTION
PO Box 4369, Medford, Oregon 97504

WHO WERE THESE STRANGE BEINGS?

They were called the Grelvi. Who were these strange other-worldly creatures— and what was the mysterious secret of their shadow world in the vast depths of the Venusian oceans? George Kerrick had come to Venus looking for adventure, but he would soon find himself involved in the mystery of these strange creatures. Kerrick was bound and determined to find the answers and more—even if it ultimately led to his own death!

Edmond Hamilton is one of the most beloved writers in the field of science fiction during the talent-rich 20th Century. "Men of the Morning Star" is another one of his "buckle-your-seatbelts" interplanetary joy rides.

FOR A COMPLETE SECOND NOVEL, TURN TO PAGE 79

CAST OF CHARACTERS

GEORGE KERRICK

He was just a working man who came to Venus looking to have a working adventure. He had no idea that his adventure would involve saving the planet.

THANE

He'd lived on Venus for 23 years. He sought to protect it and its population from the greedy fools who would destroy it for profit.

THE LAWMAKER

Head of the ruling class, the Sulvini. He cared little for anything except his own wealth and comfort—including his own daughter

MR. WELKER

Head of "The Company," whose mining operations brought in vast wealth while Venusians suffered. Would planetary law catch up to him?

LELLA

Being the beautiful daughter of The Lawmaker had its rewards, but her heart went out to the plight of the working Venusians.

THE GRELVI

Mythical sea creatures of Venus---but are they really mythical and what will they do to protect their territory?

CHAPTER ONE

THE KNIFE CAME out of the fog behind Kerrick, so that he didn't see it until it went past his ear and clattered against the dripping stone of the sea-wall ahead. The metal glittered nastily in the dim light of an oil-wood torch at the corner.

Operating on sheer physical instinct, Kerrick bent over and made a clumsy leap sideways. He was a little drunk, and he had been until this minute in a mild peaceful state where the inner fog nicely balanced the outer one and he could forget how long it seemed since he had seen the sun and the stars and smelled a clean cold wind. Now fear came with a wild shock.

Someone was trying to kill him. And he had not the faintest idea why.

He floundered in close to a warehouse wall, where the dim light was dimmer and the fog was clotted thick. He tried to see who was behind him on the quay, but all he could see was the mist rolling in slow waves from the tideless sea. The three torches that marked the tavern he had just left made a golden blob against the mist, which was tinged with the color of the purple night of Venus where cloud and sea, land and air are never quite dark, any more than they are ever quite light by day.

He listened, and he heard the faint, small, furtive sounds of bare-footed men moving lightly over the moss-grown paving stones, toward him.

The stone wall of the warehouse was solid to where the

Men Of The Morning Star

by
Edmond Hamilton

Who were these strange beings? And what was the secret of their shadow world in alien ocean depths? Did they mean death to Kerrick?

torch burned, marking the end of the quay and lighting the huge, vaguely anthropomorphic god who sat at the corner of the breakwater and peered eternally out to sea. Kerrick was unarmed and sober enough to know that he was just a little too foggy to fight effectively. He began to run for the corner. Beyond it the road led between the city and the sea to the Company plant, a distance of less than a mile. He might not be able to make the plant, but he would have a chance to dodge and hide until his head cleared and he could at least fight back.

The padding footsteps behind him came faster, and now he heard voices whispering.

The dim glare of the torch lit up his tight red tunic like aflame. The light seemed as bright as a midday sun as he passed under it. The flesh of his back quivered, anticipating a thrown blade.

It did not come. Kerrick darted around the corner, dizzy with relief.

Two men stood dim and sinister in the fog, squarely in his road.

And now he understood that this was no chance encounter. These men had circled around to cut him off in case he escaped that first knife. The whole pack of them must have been in position and waiting for him when he left the tavern. The two in front of him were Venusians, tall white-skinned men with pale eyes and albinoid hair, wearing the short loose garment common to the lower classes. They held drawn knives.

They sprang at him.

Kerrick whirled and ran across the quay. The thrown knife still lay where it had fallen. He picked it up and turned, backing into the angle of the sea-wall where the god sat. He set his shoulders against the broad stone buttocks, worn smooth as glass by a thousand generations of passing fishermen stroking them for luck. He held the knife out like a sword in front of him and snarled at the shapes corning toward him in the blue fog.

"What do you want with me?" he demanded, in his painful copybook Venusian.

And one of the men said slowly, so that he would understand, "We will kill you and throw your body before the palace gates."

There was a cold implacable hatred in the man's voice that affected Kerrick more than the threat, though that was unpleasant enough.

"But why?" he said in astonishment. "I've done no wrong, I'm a diver-technician—"

"You're a *litharni*", the man said. "Some day all the *litharni* will be dead, and the Sulvini with them."

Litharni meant roughly *wearers of the red,* and the Sulvini were the local ruling class, Kerrick realized that he was in the middle of something bigger than a mere matter of murder for robbery, or even murder for fun.

The red tunic was the Company uniform. The Company was Jones & Lansing Sea-Mines, Inc. A couple of centuries ago on Earth, having used up all available land resources, men had begun to mine the sea water of its dilute but incalculable wealth, taking from it not only gold and silver but vital supplies of uranium, copper, manganese, and a dozen more minerals essential to keep Earth's vast industries going and her food supply adequate. Then when interplanetary flight had been established, and the seas of Venus were found to be infinitely richer in minerals than the seas of Earth, it was inevitable that outfits like Jones & Lansing would set up their great pumps and vats and atomic fractionators on the misty beaches and start sucking the riches from these endless oceans.

They operated under direct agreement with the Sulvini, the rulers. Kerrick in his innocence had supposed that everybody was happy about the arrangement. The Company tunic, indeed, was designed to set Company employees apart from such Terran riff-raff as could be found in any port, and in the few weeks Kerrick had been here he had found that it was a guarantee of red-carpet treatment almost anywhere in the city.

It seemed that there were some who did not feel that way about it at all.

THEY CLOSED IN ON HIM out of the fog, padding on their hard bare feet over the wet stones. The air was warm, rank with the smell of weed and water, stifling on the lungs. Kerrick sweated and his heart hammered. There were five men. They all had knives but one.

His back and sides were protected in the angle of the wall

but that was not going to do him much good. Their superior numbers would simply pin him eventually against the stones and they could take turns cutting him up at their leisure. His position was more of a trap than an advantage. If he could get through them, clear of them, he might be able to run—

He took a deep breath and charged straight for the one unarmed man.

As Kerrick had hoped, the man flinched aside from the long blade and bumped into the man beside him, fouling his weapon-arm and creating a momentary gap in the line. Kerrick plunged into it, swinging his knife in great slashing arcs. The Venusians avoided him easily. They let him get almost though between them and then one of them hooked a foot around his ankle from behind and brought him crashing down on the oozy stones. The knife flew out of his hand. This is it, he thought, with the breath going out of him in a rush and the blue mist turning darker around his ringing head. This is it, and oh God what a hell of a place to die and not even know why you're doing it.

He wrenched himself over in a sudden fury, onto his back with his knees pulled up and his arms bent to protect his face. They were already on top of him. He kicked upward with both feet and caught one of them in the belly. The man gasped and dropped away backward, but there were still four others. Kerrick saw a hand with a knife in it swinging in hard toward his throat. He caught the wrist and pulled it up and over and the man was yanked forward off balance. He fell on top of Kerrick, and Kerrick grappled with him, thinking, I can kill at least one to keep me company—

Hard bare feet kicked him in the side of the head, in the ribs and groin. His grip weakened. He felt the man pulled away from him and nothing was between him and their blades, no possible further stalling of the inevitable.

And then he heard the voice speaking.

It spoke Venusian, liquid and pure, without accent, but somehow Kerrick knew it was an Earthman's voice. It spoke with a quiet authority. Kerrick tried to see through the fog and daze of pain. He thought the Venusians had drawn back a little away from him. They were arguing heatedly, but the voice of the Earthman kept saying, something that sounded like, "This is not the way." And they were hesitating to kill Kerrick.

Kerrick struggled up to his hands and knees and he saw the Earthman in the light of the oil-wood torch, clouded in the blue fog so that he was more a stark face and a pair of shoulders and two strong hands than a whole man. The face was bleached white as a native's by sunless years, cured to a leathery leanness by wind and water, a half geometric structure of strong horizontal bones with the vertical planes of the cheeks sunk a little inward and the eyes deeply shadowed. He wore no hat. His hair was thick and roughly cut. It had been black but was now quite gray.

Kerrick rubbed the back of his wrist across his mouth to get the blood and the moss out of it. "For God's sake," he said to the Earthman, "tell them I haven't done them any harm—"

The Earthman said curtly, "Shut up." He continued to speak to the Venusians, who continued to argue, though obviously with respect. Most of the talk was too rapid for Kerrick to follow, even if his head had been clear. The Earthman pointed out past the sitting god, to where the dark water breathed and glimmered in the purple gloom. The Venusians looked that way too. Then they looked uneasily at each other, and finally at Kerrick, and one of them smiled, a very unpleasant smile as though he would be happy to forego Kerrick's murder so that something much nastier could happen to him. Then they sheathed their knives and went away, one of them assisting the one Kerrick had kicked and who was still unable to stand straight.

Kerrick was able to stand. He watched them go with a mixed feeling of rage and shivering relief.

"Thanks," he said to the Earthman. "Another second and—what the devil was the matter with them? Why kill me?"

The Earthman looked at him. His eyes were dark, very keen, very kind, and yet with a certain paradoxical hint of ruthlessness about them. His attitude toward Kerrick seemed to be one of speculation, as though he had pulled something up in a net and wasn't sure yet what it was.

"Could you use a drink?" he said.

"Damn right I could," said Kerrick. Reaction was melting him down inside like so much wax. He started toward the golden halo of light in front of the tavern on the quay. The Earthman caught his arm.

"Haven't you had enough for one night? How long have you been on Venus?"

"Twelve weeks, mostly on Island 6. This is my first real leave."

THE EARTHMAN GRUNTED. "And doesn't the Company teach you to stay in the city when you want relaxation?"

"I think they mentioned it. But I wanted to see—"

"Native life in the raw. Of course."

"Well, you don't have to make it sound so snooty," Kerrick said, getting mad all over again. "I wasn't sneering at them. If I'm going to be stuck here for three solid years I want to—"

"Let's go get that drink," said the Earthman, cutting him off. "This way."

He led off along the inland road toward the city. Kerrick followed, still too upset to be more than feebly resentful of the man's rudeness. Besides, the man had saved his life, and he did want a drink, and above all an explanation.

"How long have you been here?" he asked.

"Twenty-three years."

A drifter, thought Kerrick. A renegade. And yet he didn't look like one.

"My name's Kerrick. George Kerrick. I'm a diver-technician—"

"With the Company. Yes. My name is Thane. If I ever had another one I've forgotten it. I'm a diver-technician too, in a way. Marine biologist. To your right there—yes, right through that crack. This is a short cut."

Kerrick slid into an alley no more than three feet wide between two high stone tenements. Nearly everything on Venus was built of stone because any other material washed, rotted or rusted away in the sweating dampness and torrential rains. The alley was extremely dark and smelly. Kerrick could make out a dim glow at the far end. He hurried toward it and was glad when he came out into a long narrow courtyard, overhung on four sides with tiers of balconies and lighted both by torches at the low tunnel entrance opposite the narrow alley and by lamps inside the windows. There was a beehive murmur of voices and laughter from the apartments and the flat populous roofs. The omnipresent fog curled gently over all.

Thane guided him up ladder like steps with the rungs worn into hollows in the center.

"You wanted to see native life," he said. "I'll show you some. This is my home when I come in from the reefs. I've known these people for a generation now. I consider them my family—my *other* family," He paused. "I have two of them, you know."

Probably a native wife and some half-bred kids out on the reefs, Kerrick thought, and decided it was none of his business. But he wondered how even a marine biologist—if Thane really was one—could live for twenty-three years in the godforsaken and still only superficially known maze of reefs and weed and half-submerged islands that made the shallow Venusian oceans impossible of navigation for anything but the small native craft.

Thane motioned him onto a balcony about midway up. A brace of floss-haired children were curled like puppies on a heap of soft rugs at the back of it, sound asleep. There was a curious kind of trident with round knobs instead of prongs hung up on hooks above the door.

"Go in," said Thane, and Kerrick stooped his head under the low arch.

The room inside was spacious and clean. There was a raised and hooded fireplace in one corner, some low chests, tanned skins to soften the red stone walls and bright woven rugs on the stone floor. Along one wall ran a raised platform that was sitting space for all by day and sleeping space by night. There were four people and a baby on it now.

Kerrick still had trouble trying to judge the ages of Venusians, who did not seem to develop as many wrinkles as Earthfolk. But it didn't take much ingenuity to figure that one of the couples were the grandparents of the baby and the other its mother and father. The older couple looked as though they had a lot of good years in them yet. The two men were playing some gambling game and drinking the pale-brown mild intoxicant that looked like flat beer and tasted like nothing under the sun. The women were doing something with the baby. They all turned toward the door, their expressions changing swiftly from welcome for Thane to the exact opposite at the sight of Kerrick and his red tunic.

The men got up sharply, letting the pieces fall.

CHAPTER TWO

THANE SAID, speaking slowly now so that Kerrick could follow, "I have promised this man a drink for his body and words for his soul. He was set upon near the Watching God and almost killed. He desires to know why."

"Anyone in the harbor quarter could have told him," said the older man. "Why bring him here?"

"I'm not sure," said Thane, smiling. "It was a thought that came to me. This is a diver, a man of the sea himself, and he has only been a *litharni* for twelve weeks. Perhaps there is hope for him."

Both men grunted as though they doubted it.

Kerrick said grimly, "Ordinarily I'm damned if I'll stay where I'm not wanted, but this time I'm staying. Five men just tried to cut my throat. I want to know what their grievance was and whether it's likely to happen again, and what the devil goes on. So you can't insult me."

"Well, then," said the older man grudgingly, "sit down. You're Thane's guest and so I refrain from throwing you out bodily." He turned to speak to the older woman, who rose with a perfectly stony countenance and fetched clay cups and a jug.

Thane made the introductions. "This is Donavel, whose trident hangs there—" He pointed to a second round-tipped trident hung above the door inside, and Kerrick understood that this was a symbol of headship, "—and Verilan, his son. They are herdsmen."

"Herdsmen," said Kerrick. "You mean the fellows in the kayaks?"

Now he remembered where he had seen tridents like that

before. When he was out on Island 6 several men had gone past in tiny boats that could be rolled over without taking water. They had been furiously active, going with a rush and a cry after a school of great fishy creatures with crimson scales, and they had used tridents to prod the brutes on and keep them together. It had been explained to Kerrick that they were herdsmen bringing their charges back from seasonal pasturage in the weed-beds. It had seemed like a slimy job to Kerrick, but he had become used to eating the fish, which was pretty good. And it stood to reason that on a planet where the largest single land area was only slightly larger than New Zealand the people would have to look to the oceans for their food supply.

Thane said, "The fellows in the kayaks, yes. Drink, Kerrick, and Donavel will tell you why the *litharni* are not loved."

Donavel leaned forward. Like his son he was lean and muscular, with a shrewd eye and capable hands.

"You are spoilers," he said to Kerrick. "Like the Sulvini, and like the great solar tide that takes and never gives again. At first we thought you Earthmen were good, the beginning of a new day for us, who are not so ignorant as the Sulvini hope to keep us. A few of us have travelled, a few of us have videos and talking books. Knowledge is hard to keep out. So we believed. Now the Sulvini will have to change their ways a little and there will be schools and medical places and more contact with the outside. But has this been so? Hah! The Sulvini grow fat on royalties from the mining lease, and the Company grows fat on minerals taken from our seas. While we—"

"We," said Verilan quietly, "will starve one day." And he looked at his wife and baby.

Kerrick shook his head. "But why?"

"The Company spreads and spreads. You say you are a

diver, you know the sea. Then you must know how your planets are changing the currents, killing the sea growths, altering the temperature of the water, spreading pollution from your wastes. The fishing fleets must go farther and farther to find a catch. Our coastal pasturage is vanishing and our beasts die because the chemical balance is upset. The men who farm the weed-crops are driven beyond their agreed boundaries, and still our rulers the Sulvini lease more islands to the Company and squander their millions on luxuries while we get nothing. Now. Do you understand why we hate the *litharni*?"

Feeling uncomfortable, guilty and resentful all at once, Kerrick was about to say something when the older woman spoke for the first time in a voice sharp with long-pent anger.

"Greed will betray you all," she said. "You already trespass on the Grelvi seas. The Sulvini have forgotten how those boundaries were set in ancient times, and the Company does not know. But the Grelvi will teach you both!"

"I hope not," said Thane, and his face was suddenly very grave.

"Listen," said Kerrick, "I'm sorry if things are bad for you. I didn't know the sea-mining operations were making it tough. But we—the *litharni*—are in about the same spot. We have to work for a living, and we have to go where the bosses tell us. We don't have anything to do with running the Company or making its policies. We never saw either Jones or Lansing, and we don't even see Welker—he's the Company manager—unless he calls us on the carpet for something, So if you killed every one of us it wouldn't change anything. And who are the Grelvi, anyway?"

"Tell him, Thane," said a new voice from the doorway. Kerrick started and turned around, and so did everybody else. The voice was a woman's, with ringing quality in it, but all Kerrick could see was a tallish form covered from head to foot in a coarse cloak of broad yellow weed-leaves, cured and tied by the stems like thatch to keep the rain off.

"Lella!" cried Thane, and jumped up to go to her. The Venusians rose smiling, but were more shyly respectful than Thane, who took hold of a white hand that appeared through the thatch, and shook it warmly.

THE PERSON INSIDE the cloak said, "I heard you had come back, Thane. I got away the first minute I could. But I didn't expect to find a *litharni* here."

Thane glanced at Kerrick, who was standing quietly watching. "It's an experiment," said Thane. "I'm not sure how it will turn out."

"It's all right," said Lella, "I want to talk to him,"

She rustled the thatched cloak and Thane lifted it away from her.

Kerrick's eyes opened wide.

This was a woman of the Sulvini, a very young one, hardly more than a girl, but with a vitality and loveliness that were startling to come upon so abruptly and without warning. Her skin had the white translucence of pearl, and her body was just about perfect under a clinging chiton of some mist-colored stuff. The women of the herders wore their long pale hair in a loose knot, and they were handsome enough with their clear features and their sea-green eyes. Lella's eyes were the color of amethysts and her hair was dyed—after the custom of the Sulvini women—to match them, cut short and curled in feathery curls around her head.

Kerrick tried to remember the proper Venusian form for greeting a high-born lady, and all he could do was stammer.

Lella laughed. "You seem almost human. How long have you been a *litharni*?"

"Only twelve weeks," said Kerrick, and for some reason the words came out with a sound of apology for having been one even that long.

Thane placed Lella's cloak over a chest and went out onto the balcony. Kerrick heard him speak to someone— probably, Kerrick thought, Lella's servant. She would hardly have come alone into the harbor quarter at night.

Lella sat down on the platform, where Donavel and the others practically enthroned her. She talked to them as to old friends and admired the baby. Kerrick shifted from one foot to the other, trying not to stare. He had seen Sulvini women around in the city, of course, but never so close, and few of them had looked anything like this.

Thane came back in, looking worried. "Harn says he thinks someone followed you."

"Harn is worse than an old woman for seeing danger in every shadow," Lella said, waving a hand in affectionate scorn.

"Just the same," said Thane, and spoke to Verilan, who thrust a long knife in his belt and went outside.

"There are some people who disapprove of my revolutionary activities," Lella explained to Kerrick. "They would dearly love to catch me at them, so that I might be legally locked up and married off." She made a grimace of profound distaste and was about to say more when Thane stopped her, shaking his head.

Lella smiled, "But this young man has honest eyes, Thane. I would trust—oh, well, of course you're right." Her face became serious. "Let us hear about the Grelvi. I know that only a crisis would bring you in from the reefs at this time of the year."

Thane turned to Kerrick. "You said you had been on Island 6 most of your twelve weeks?"

"That's right. It's an old installation, of course, and diving there is routine. They were just breaking me in. I believe they always do that with new divers—team them up with a veteran on an old plant so as to teach them what to look out for."

"Was there any talk about Island 10?"

"Some. It's the newest one and the farthest out. I don't think they've even started construction there yet."

"And you never heard of the Grelvi?"

"No."

"You will. Island 10 is on their border."

Kerrick frowned, trying to remember his Venusian geography. "I don't remember the map showing anything but a mess of reefs and weed in that area, and little hunks of rock like Island 10. Is there a big island there I missed?"

"No, There's no big island. There's no land worthy of the name for a thousand miles. The Grelvi have a different kind of country." His face had become intent and grave, somehow conveying a very solid threat.

"They're a quiet folk. They haven't needed to go to war for centuries, not since the boundaries were set. They don't mix with the land-dwellers, and everybody has more or less forgotten about them—"

"Not everybody," said Lella, interrupting. "Donavel hasn't forgotten. Neither have the fishermen and the weed farmers. Only the Sulvini have forgotten."

"You mean the Sulvini are leasing sites to the Company that they don't really have title to?" asked Kerrick.

"In the case of Island 10," said Thane, "yes."

Kerrick said slowly, "That could make an awful lot of trouble for everybody."

He was a little staggered at the thought of just how much trouble it could make.

"And Island 10 is only the first step," said Lella. There was a bitter note in her voice. She turned those brilliant amethyst eyes on Kerrick and went on, forcefully. "I will tell you, *litharni*, that all of my class are not bad, that all of us are not fools, that some of us do not like what is being done to our own people. Unfortunately there are not enough of us to overthrow the party in power—"

"Without help," muttered Donavel, and Lella glanced at him in quick alarm.

"Hush," she said, "I was about to say 'by vote', especially so long as the sea-mineral royalties buy palaces and ropes of jewels for so many. And so things must get worse before they get better. Perhaps, Thane, your beloved Grelvi will be the answer, if not for Island 10, then for Island 11 and Island 12—oh, yes. Welker has been talking terms already with the Lawmaker."

"Lawmaker" was the title of the local petty king.

"But," said Kerrick, "if that's true, all you have to do is tell Welker—you'd have to have proof, of course, which I imagine you have or could get—"

"I gave Welker proof a year ago," said Thane quietly. "He told me to get back to my reefs and my unsavory relationships and spare him my crackpot interference."

THINKING IT just possible that Welker might have known what he was talking about, Kerrick said,

"Couldn't you send a message to the big bosses on Earth? They'd at least investigate."

"Would they? With all that money involved? I wonder. And anyway, the Lawgiver personally reads and censors all messages sent out from the city. I don't think Welker would let me use the Company radio, either."

In an abrupt rush of words that surprised Kerrick by their violence, Thane continued.

"Perhaps that's why I brought you here, to pass on this information to someone in the Company so that if anything happens to me there may still be a chance of getting the facts to someone who will listen."

"Are you expecting something to happen?"

"It would not cause me the slightest surprise. So remember this night."

"I'm not likely to forget it," Kerrick said, and looked at Lella.

There was a sudden scream of childish fright, an outcry and a scurry of feet from the balcony.

Instantly Thane and Donavel sprang to the door, two steps behind the children's mother. Kerrick hesitated for a second, Lella had stiffened where she sat and he was shocked to see an expression of genuine terror in her eyes.

He followed Thane and Donavel onto the balcony.

He almost collided with a large muscular stranger who was on his way in. Thane said,

"This is Harn—he'll stay with Lella."

The woman was hustling the two sobbing little ones inside, her face white. Verilan was already halfway to the roof. The others followed him, scrambling up the worn stone steps past balconies filled with curious craning heads. There was a babble of voices. Thane said over his shoulder.

"A man crept down from the roof behind Harn and got into the balcony through the outer arch." Apparently he meant that the man had swung himself over the ledge of the balcony above, a nerve-shattering feat with that drop to the stones below. "Verilan was watching the courtyard from farther down. If the man hadn't wakened the children we might never have known he was there."

Then somebody had followed Lella. Kerrick was angry. He didn't know why. It was none of his business—

But she had looked so frightened.

They emerged onto the roof. It was as wide and flat as a ballpark, comprising several tenements built side by side. There were channels to carry off the rain and lumpish-looking gods perched at the corners and at intervals along the parapets, wherever landlords or tenants had had the pious whim to put them. There were also a number of people there, watching with cheerful excitement and quarreling loudly about exactly what they had seen and where the stranger had disappeared to. Donavel and his son went rapidly among them, peering at them in the dim light and asking names.

A sheet of lightning flared across the southern sky and a wind sprang up, rolling the mist in sullen masses across the roofs.

Donavel came back. "These are all tenants. They disagree, every one swearing to a different thing. The man was a Venusian and he wore a dark-colored tunic and he crossed the roof. More than that I can't say. All we can do is search."

Thane nodded, "I'll go this way." He glanced at Kerrick. "You'd better go back down."

"No," said Kerrick, "I think I'll stay."

"As you will. Suppose you try the north side. It'll storm soon. If we don't catch our man before then he'll be gone for good."

They scattered out in different directions. Kerrick ran across the weather-beaten stones, feeling uneasily that this night was going to prove the unluckiest one of his life so far. He almost wished Thane had left him alone on the quay. Then he thought that if all this stuff about the greedy Sulvini granting leases to other peoples' islands was true, everybody in the Company was in trouble and he was better off to know it.

And Welker—Jonathan C. Welker, the efficient Great Stone Face in the Front Office—was he in on it, too? Thane had said so. He had even implied that Welker might not be above having him killed to shut his mouth about the outer islands.

And of course Thane might be no more a crackpot, and Lella an earnest kid mixed up in an illusory cause. But—

Kerrick had a strong idea that it might be best for him to talk to this spy—who had looked in upon a scene of which he was a part and would inevitably report same—and find out who the man was working for and why.

It occurred to him in passing that he still had no clear idea of who or what the Grelvi were.

The wind was strengthening, blowing in huge gusts. The fog was torn, rolled, and swept away, and suddenly the sea, the harbor, and the city stood clear. Out on the dark water the lightning danced and flared. The crowded huddle of tenements of which this one was a part rimmed all the curving beaches and ran back over the low-lying ground— seasonally flooded by the solar tides—until abruptly the ground rose and the villas of the Sulvini showed on the terraced hillsides, set wide apart among flowering trees. Over all, on the very height of the hill, the ancient fortress of the Lawmakers hulked like a monument to a ruder age, its gaunt towers built all of black stone. To his right, on a jutting promontory a mile or more down the coast, Kerrick could see the flat white plasticoid buildings and towered monstrosities of the Company plant, glimmering in the lightning-glare.

The first rain came and in a matter of seconds the tenants had vanished off the roof.

Kerrick could hear them laughing and chattering down the steps. He doubted that the stranger was among them. He would be sure to be noticed. Either he had already got away or he was still hiding somewhere on the roofs.

Wind and rain drove across the city and now everything was obscured again. The lightning was tremendous, the thunder gargantuan. Kerrick went down almost to his hands and knees to avoid being blown away. The downpour made it difficult to breathe, almost impossible to see.

There was a row of stone godlings perched along the parapet, a little distance away. The lightning showed them at intervals, briefly, stark in the purplish glare.

A particularly vivid flash caught one of the smaller godlings in the act of rising and running away.

CHAPTER THREE

KERRICK WAS on the man before he had gone three paces. They fell together on the stones, rolling and thrashing in the inch or so of water that had already accumulated. Another flash showed him the Venusian's face, white and startled. It was a nasty face, not at all the kind that Kerrick wanted overseeing anything he personally was connected with. He leaned back and gave it a good solid smash with his first.

It wasn't enough. Not nearly enough. The man was as strong as a tiger and this was obviously not the first time in his life he had had to fight. He went for the inevitable long knife in his girdle, Kerrick pounded him in the face again and managed to snatch the knife out and throw it away. Then he was caught in an explosion of fists and knees, feet and elbows.

The man was savagely anxious to shake him off and get away. Kerrick hung on. In a way he enjoyed it. The knife was not his weapon, but he had always been handy with his fists at need and he had a powerful load of resentments to work off.

They rolled and pounded and flailed together in the midst of the storm, while the gutters began to roar like little Niagara's. The man's flesh was slippery with the wet, hard to hold onto. Twice he almost broke away and twice Kerrick stopped him, the second time with a fine kick under the ribs that knocked the wind out of him just long enough for Kerrick to scramble on top of him and get a strong grip an his rubbery neck.

"Who sent you?" he shouted, trying to bellow over the noise of the storm. He banged the Venusian's head up and down against the stones and the running water splashed. "What are you trying to find out?"

The man rolled under his knees, trying to get away. In the lightning flares his eyes and his bared teeth glittered like an animal's. He panted heavily but he did not speak.

Kerrick pressed dawn harder on his throat. "Answer me!"

The man appeared to be strangling, between Kerrick's grip and the water that was pouring into his mouth and nose. He made frantic gestures. Kerrick let up on him. There was no sign of Thane and the others. Either they were still searching their areas of roof or else they had dived for shelter like wise men, giving up the search as hopeless in this storm.

The Venusian gasped, "This is—a private matter, *litharni*. Not your affair."

"I'm making it mine. Who sent you?"

"The Lawmaker."

Kerrick laughed. "Try again."

The man seemed genuinely angry. "You're a fool, *litharni*. You ask for ill fortune. The Lawmaker is Lella's father."

That rocked Kerrick back on his heels. "The Lawmaker?" he repeated. "Lella's father?" Things jarred abruptly into a new and even less happy perspective.

And now the Venusian laughed, silently, while his hands rubbed at his bruised throat.

"Lella's father," he said. "And he doesn't like her choice of friends. Poor *litharni*!"

His hand darted suddenly into the breast of his tunic and came out with a lumpy stringy thing that Kerrick barely saw before it was whipped across his head with such force that he thought lightning must have struck him. In the next second he felt himself thrown off. He made a blind effort to get up and go after the man but when his sight cleared the Venusian was already out of reach and running like the wind.

The next flash of lightning showed the roof empty.

KERRICK TURNED slowly and walked away, holding his head, wondering what the devil had hit him.

Thane and the others had come looking for him, having drawn blanks themselves. He explained what had happened in about three words, while they stood with their heads together and the water washed over their ankles and the storm got incredibly worse. Then they fought their way down the steps to the refuge of the apartment.

Lella was still there. Kerrick faced her. "Is the Lawmaker your father?"

"Yes," she said, "He is."

"That makes things just fine," said Kerrick sourly, and looked at Thane. "Thanks so much for bringing me here. You'd have done better just to let them cut my throat."

"Never mind that," said Thane grimly. "Tell me exactly what happened."

Kerrick told him, right down to the ignominious finish. "I didn't see what the damned thing was," he concluded, "he hauled it out so fast, and he gave me a royal bang on the head with it and then ran. And that's all."

Thane grunted, frowning. He reached into his own tunic—which was the loose Venusian type—and brought out a woven metallic cord about two feet long, very strong and pliable, and furnished with two lumps of lead or something equally heavy at each end.

Kerrick said instantly, "Yes, that was it."

"And he said the Lawmaker sent him to spy on Lella?"

"Yes."

"He was lying," Thane said, and swung the weighted cord between his hands.

"How do you know?" demanded Kerrick.

It was Lella who explained.

"That is a strangler's weapon. Thane has his own reasons for carrying one, but among our people, only criminals have use for them. Now, it is true that my father and I are at sword's points. But not he nor any of the Sulvini would hire a criminal to spy on their women."

"That is so," said Donavel, and all the others nodded.

"All right," said Kerrick. "Then who did send him?"

Thane glanced uneasily at Lella. "We don't know."

"But we can make a shrewd guess, can't we, Thane?" she said, and her face was practically incandescent with anger. "We must tell the *litharni*—Kerrick? Yes, Kerrick. It would not be fair not to warn him."

She spoke directly to Kerrick.

"Your Mr. Welker has been bargaining for me with my father."

For some reason difficult to explain, this outraged Kerrick. Perhaps it was because he did not like Welker very well. Their contacts had necessarily been few and far from intimate, but the man struck him as a thoroughly cold fish and he was not popular among the employees. Or perhaps it was because it seemed unthinkable that anyone like Lella should be bargained for like an animal or a piece of property.

He said, "You think the spy was working for Welker?"

"You've only been among us for twelve weeks," Lella said. "Our customs are perhaps strange to you. I am a Sulvini, and so I may not be forced to marry against my will—*unless* I am caught in some crime against the state or against the person of another Sulvini. Then I lose all independent rights and may be dealt with at the discretion of the Lawmaker."

"I see," said Kerrick, "And Welker figures that if he can

prove you're in some kind of conspiracy he can get you that way."

Kerrick discovered that he hated Mr. Welker very deeply.

Thane had been talking earnestly with Donavel and the others. Now he said to Kerrick.

"You had better go now. If you're questioned about tonight, say that I brought you here after that business on the quay simply to see that you were all right—which is the truth—and then play dumb about the rest. You didn't understand most of the talk, and you thought the girl was the daughter of the house, and the man you caught a robber. Do this for us as well as yourself. You do owe me a debt."

Kerrick grunted, "And what about Island 10?"

"I'll leave that to your conscience. If the time comes when you think you must do something about it, you have the information. If you need proof, go to the Grelvi. In the meantime, watch out for yourself. Times are approaching a crisis here and the *litharni* will feel it. Stay away from the quays and dark places."

THANE GAVE a brief wry smile and held out the weighed cord.

"You'd better have this. It may serve you with the Grelvi too—they know it's mine. See here." He showed Kerrick how the weights were stamped with a curious little symbol. "That's their writing. Most of my belongings are marked with it, so that even strange Grelvi let me alone."

Kerrick hesitated, and Thane said, "Take it. I'm going to tackle the Lawmaker himself in the morning and I can't use it on him."

"Well," said Kerrick. "All right."

He took the thing and stowed it under his belt.

Lella was talking to the women. Their faces were all grim and strained and the young mother kept looking anxiously at her brood. Harn, the big man who was Lella's servant and guardian, brought the stiff cloak and started to bundle her into it.

Kerrick went to her and said two rather foolish things. "I'm sorry," he said, and, "Be careful."

She seemed to understand what he meant, because she smiled and held out her hand to him and said, "You, too. If you ever need help, come to me and I will do what I can." Then she said darkly, "Unless—"

Kerrick pressed her hand. It felt warm in his with a beautiful warmth that went all through him and made him dizzy. And he said something even more foolish.

He said, "Unless you are the one who needs help. In that case, come to me."

She looked at him deeply and steadily for a moment, ceasing to smile. Then Harn took her away and a few minutes later Kerrick himself was sloshing forlornly through the rain in the empty courtyard below, wondering in just what way he would be able to help Lella against the combined power of her father and the Company under the guidance of J. C. Welker.

As he started under the low arch he turned and glanced back at the apartment he had just left.

It was already pitch dark.

He shivered and hurried through the storm-scoured streets and out along the road to the Company plant.

He was awakened next morning, in his small functional living cubicle that was just a bit reminiscent of a prison cell, by the impersonal but commanding voice of the intercom.

"George Kerrick," it said.

"Please report as soon as possible to Mr. Welker's office."

CHAPTER FOUR

MR. WELKER'S OFFICE was at the top of what was known as the Exec Tower, a twenty-story structure rising above the north end of the flat main building that contained the living quarters, kitchens, hospital, recreation center, and some of the clerical departments. Exec housed the computers, the records storage banks, and the centers where current data from all operating plants such as Island 6 were processed and evaluated. LEGAL and PLANNING were here, and also ENGINEERING. So were the executive suites, unoccupied except during the visits of Mr. Jones and Mr. Lansing, and Mr. Welker's only slightly less sumptuous apartments.

The office itself was large and handsomely furnished in a sparse, stern way. The walls on all four sides were windows, so that Welker could sit up here like an old-time captain on the bridge of his ship, overlooking the whole plant from the primary pumping station where the sea-water was forced into the great vats, through the seemingly endless rows of fractionating tubes where the last atom of each mineral element was extracted from the water, to the bulbous structure housing the endpoint control system which fed back data in a continuous stream to the input control, keeping the whole cycle going. Beyond the plant, you could see on one side the gaunt black hulk of the fortress squatting on its hill, and on the other side the sea, a quiet vastness of pearl-gray silk by day, dappled with shifting tints of rose and purple and lavender and green and gold from floating weed or colored strata beneath the shallow water, or from equally fleeting tints in the cloudy sky. At the horizon line, sea and sky met in a luminous smother of mist, so that you had always the feeling of being imprisoned at the heart of a pale opal, or a pearl. It was remarkable

Kerrick had this feeling. He doubted that Welker felt anything except the powerful smooth forward-driving force of success, which meant getting what he wanted—higher production, hig- her pay, more praise, more power.

And Lella.

Welker was a tall big fine-looking man. His eyes were a bright hard blue and his features were likable at first glance, giving the impression of intelligence and a kind of alert humor. At second glance the essential coldness of the man became apparent, in the way he spoke and thought, in his total lack of any real warmth of friendliness. Not that Kerrick expected Welker to embrace him and invite him up to dinner. But Welker had a way of looking through people as though he considered them not worth the time it would take to notice them.

This time, when Kerrick walked in the office door, Welker noticed him. And Kerrick felt his insides coil together in a tight knot. *I'm in trouble*, he thought, *right up to my neck*. And then he thought angrily, If the so-and-so jumps me I'll break his jaw for him.

Welker did not jump him. He smiled and said easily, "Good morning, Kerrick—you know Truby, don't you?"

Gil Truby, a lean little man who was a senior diver and one of the Company's best, got up off the edge of a chair where he had been sitting stiffly. He nodded to Kerrick, who said, "Hello, Gil."

Welker continued to look at Kerrick with a sharp icy stare that was quite independent of his smile and his pleasant voice.

"I've had excellent reports on you from Island 6," he said. "You seem to have passed your apprenticeship with flying colors."

He stopped and seemed to expect an answer, so Kerrick said, "I'm glad to hear it."

"In fact," said Welker. "I hear so well of you that I'm going to give you to Truby."

It sounded all right. The only thing wrong was the expression on Truby's face.

"But," said Truby. "But, Mr. Welker! That's totally unexplored bottom. A new man—"

"I'm sure Kerrick win learn rapidly." Welker's smile broadened for one brief moment and then was gone, and now his hard blue eyes were fastened on Truby, daring him to make any further protests. "I know it's short notice, but I want both of you on the survey boat going out this noon."

Truby hesitated. Then he said, "Yes, Mr. Welker."

Welker looked at Kerrick.

Kerrick said carefully, "Could I ask where the survey boat is going?"

"I thought I mentioned that," Welker said. "It's going to. Island 10."

"Island 10," repeated Kerrick. His face tightened. "I see."

It figured. Welker was hardly going to make any direct reference to last night's incident, because mentioning it would admit his complicity in what had happened, a thing that would not make him any more popular with Lella and probably not with her father either. But he certainly would not want Kerrick around now. There was no telling how much the spy had heard before he was detected, and in any case Welker would make the blanket assumption that Thane and Lella and the herdsmen had outlined their viewpoints to him, probably including remarks potentially damaging to himself.

So Kerrick was being sent to Island 10, into dangerous and unknown waters, with the threat of the Grelvi added to the ever-present threat of the sea itself.

"The Company is expanding, Kerrick," Welker said, with his cold little smile, "I'm giving you the opportunity to be in the forefront of that expansion."

"Thank you," said Kerrick stiffly, looking straight at him. "Will you issue guns to the party?"

"Guns?" said Welker, surprised.

"To fight the Grelvi. I understand they claim title to Island 10, They may object to our being there."

"The Grelvi!" said Welker angrily. "You've been listening to old wives' tales. The creatures aren't human, if they exist at all—have you ever seen one, Truby?"

"No, sir."

"And how can non-human beasts lay any claim to property?"

"That would be up to the Legal Department to say, Mr. Welker," Kerrick said.

"Then you let the Legal Department worry about it."

HE PRESSED a button on his desk and the office door opened. Truby started toward it thankfully, but Kerrick stood his ground.

"Will the Legal Department protect us in case we kill some of these non-human beasts? Just in case they should be proved intelligent and the lawful owners of the island."

Welker's face was taking on a dangerous look. He leaned back in his chair and said quietly.

"Under the terms of your contract you are paid to dive, and nothing more. If you refuse an assignment I can place you under suspension for the period remaining on your contract—which means that you will not work for us nor for anyone else for three years. Are you refusing this one?"

"I wouldn't think of it," Kerrick said, and turned and walked out.

While they waited for the elevator down the hall, Truby shook his head. "And that's all you ever get, tangling with the Great Stone Face." He gave Kerrick a curious glance. "Did I detect something personal?"

Kerrick said, "Not exactly."

"Oh, well, it's none of my business. But what was all that stuff about the Grelvi?"

"Just something I heard."

The elevator came. They stepped into it and shot down.

"From where?" asked Truby.

"Fellow I met. An Earthman named Thane."

"Oh," said Truby. "Him."

"What do you mean, him?"

"He's—oh, you know." Truby made whirling motions beside his head. "A little bit touched. Been here so long he thinks he owns the place, and he's mucked around with the fish so long he thinks they talk to him."

And Kerrick reflected that that might be perfectly true, and the attitude of Donavel's family toward the Grelvi merely native superstition.

He would have liked to think so, but somehow Thane had not struck him as unbalanced at all, and Donavel was a pretty hardheaded type.

They stepped out of the elevator.

"Listen," said Kerrick abruptly, "will you do me a favor? Will you check out my equipment for me? There's something I have to do in town."

Truby hesitated and then said, "Well, all right. But if you're late we'll both catch hell."

"I won't be late," Kerrick promised, and left the building.

Away from the building the heat was tremendous. He moved as in a steam bath, through air so heavy with moisture he felt he needed gills to breathe it. He could have checked out a Company jeep but he would have had to explain why and he did not have any good explanation. So he walked, across the plant yard with the omnipresent throbbing of the pumps like a huge booming heart and out the gate, and along the road past where the sea was all roiled and fouled with the constant sucking of the great intakes.

By day the city looked older and more worn and weathered, the courtyards and narrow alleys simmering in the heat, the rooftops deserted. Children scurried about, as undaunted as young demons at play. Tall pale-haired women went on their way to the clamorous markets. Most of the men were already far out at sea, fishing or sea-herding or tending their floating farms.

Kerrick had some little difficulty finding the tenement again. When he did he ran up the worn steps in a great hurry, knowing that Donavel and Verilan would be away at sea but hoping that Thane might still be there.

He was puzzled to see Verilan's trident still on its rests over the door.

From inside there came a sound of weeping.

He pushed the door-curtain open and stepped hesitantly into the room. Verilan's young wife was huddled up on the platform with her baby in her laps and her two others on each side of her with her arms around them. They were all crying. The older woman sat by, staring grimly at nothing, a deep furrow between her brows.

Donavel's trident was still in its place, too.

"What is it?" asked Kerrick, "What's happened?"

The younger woman did not raise her head. Donavel's wife turned slowly and looked at him with a black bitter look that made him flinch.

"This morning before dawn," she said, "the soldiers of the Lawmaker came and took my husband and my son away."

"But why?" asked Kerrick, shocked.

"Do you suppose they must explain to us? Oh, no. But I

can tell you. It is because of last night, because of the spy who followed the royal daughter and saw her where she should not be, talking of things that were safer to be kept silent." Her voice rose, tight and shaking. "I told Donavel that this soft quiet way would only bring disaster. Rise and strike, I told him! Burn the Company, drag the Sulvini out of their villas and burn those too, and then the fortress. Shout the call among the fisher-folk, the sea-herds, the farmers, all the people of the quarter—they would follow, and gladly! But Thane and Lella said no, and Donavel listened to them and not to me."

She got up and took a step toward Kerrick.

"Now I tell you, *litharni*—get that red tunic out of here before some harm comes to you."

HER EYES SHONE with a light of murder. Kerrick did not blame her. It seemed that Welker must have passed on what he'd learned from his spy to the Lawmaker, doubtless concealing the way he had learned it.

"Please," said Kerrick, "I must see Thane. Where—"

"He went early to see the Lawmaker, to see if he could get Donavel and my son released. But he has not come back."

Kerrick said, "When he does come back, tell him I'm being sent out to Island 10 and—"

"Ah!" screamed the woman, "Ah—ah! The Grelvi will be waiting there for you! Feed them, *litharni*—fatten them and make them strong as they were in the old days, when the Sulvini cowered before them!"

There was something inexpressibly shocking about her sudden cry. To Kerrick, it was as though she spoke with the deep and ancient voice of this brooding planet, of whose secrets Earthmen had only touched the fringes. He was abruptly and powerfully stricken by the awareness, always before thrust tidily back into his subconscious, that he stood upon a world that was not Earth, a world unearthly.

"Then we shall see!" she cried, "Then we shall watch a slaying!"

It was only too obvious that he would get nothing more from her, and Kerrick was glad to retreat back down the steps.

As he reached the ground a strong hand fell upon his shoulder. He whirled, and then recognized the tall, strong-looking Venusian who faced him.

Harn. Lella's servant. For a moment an unreasoning hope thrilled Kerrick. Then Harn said,

"I have a message for you—from Thane."

"Thane? Where is he?"

"In the Lawmaker's prison," said Harn flatly. "I was to give his message to one of Donavel's women to bear to you, but now—"

"In prison?" Kerrick was startled. "What's the message?"

Harn said carefully, "If you want to repay your debt to me, get word somehow to the Grelvi where I am."

Kerrick felt a little staggered. He did owe Thane a debt—his life. And, ironically, the fact that Welker was sending him to Island 10 might make it easier to carry out Thane's request. But Thane hadn't known he was going out there. Why hadn't he asked Harn himself to take the message?

He asked that question, and Harn's face became utterly stony. He said, "No Venusian goes near the Grelvi unless they bid him come."

So that was it. Superstitious fear or superstitious reverence, so strong whichever it was that Thane had despaired of finding a Venusian messenger.

Kerrick asked, "What *are* the Grelvi, Harn?"

Harn gave him a level look and then said, "You have the message," and turned his back and stalked off.

From the window over Kerrick's head came the voice of

Donavel's wife still raised in muffled, bitter outcry, in wild and vengeful prophecy.

Kerrick shivered and turned away.

CHAPTER FIVE

IT WAS NIGHT on Island 10, Kerrick moved, cautious as a stalking cat and as quiet, past the row of plastic huts where the men were sleeping. Fog hung like a dense blue cloud over the island, drowning the lights until they were no more than candle-flames, muffling sound. It lay on the lungs like smoke and it smelled of strangeness, a haunting, frightening breath out of the unknown.

Kerrick thought with passionate regret of the lighted interior of the bare little hut he shared with Truby. But he kept on going, treading softly over the damp ground.

It was still. Now at night when all the noisy activities of building were shut down, the stillness was appalling. Unless there was a gale or a solar tide to drive it, there was seldom surf to pound the Venusian beaches anyway, so that to an Earthman there was always something uncanny about the quiet of the Venusian sea. But this was different. Kerrick could feel the water crowding around the tiny crescent-shaped island. He could hear it breathe, and touch, and tremble with a kind of vast eager waiting.

He passed the last of the huts and groped his way across a patch of open ground toward the beach.

Things had not been right since they had landed. On the first day he and Truby had been sent down to explore the configuration of the ocean floor on the east side of the island, so that Canforra, the engineer in charge, could decide which was the best location for his intake tubes. On that day the warm shallow waters had swarmed with the normal thousands of weird and brightly-colored creatures, swimming, creeping, and squirming among the painted mosses and gorgeous weed.

The second day they had gone down for samples of the bottom so that Canforra could decide whether the mud was rich enough in minerals to be worth the extra expense of an agitator installation. On this day every swimming and creeping and squirming thing was gone. The mossy pastures and the weed forests were empty and deserted, Kerrick and Truby had stayed close together, looking nervously around as they swam at the eerie thickets that swayed in the silent water, sensing an ominous and terrible threat lurking somewhere just out of sight.

It had stayed out of sight. But on the third day the weed began to die all around the island in a ring, and every day the ring widened, and the men who were on watch at night said they had seen strange lights moving in the water, deep down, and that far out in the fog great voices had spoken, and that there were ripplings and eddies along the beaches where there was no current to make them.

Canforra, who was an able engineer and as hard as one of his own plasticon foundations, used a few brief impolite words and told them that the installation on Island 10 was going up on schedule in spite of, all the lights and noises their imaginations could invent.

And it was going up. More and more equipment arrived every day in long strings of barges. The face of the island had already changed. On the east side a portable pumping station was in place, ready to feed the testing vats, and as Kerrick approached the beach he passed the pre-fab shed that housed the vats and the test fractionator that had arrived only today.

Lights were going inside the shed. The technicians must be working overtime to get the fractionator fully assembled and working. Kerrick skirted the building cautiously, pausing just long enough to glance through a window.

He could see the machine, much smaller than the permanent single-function ones that would replace it. It was pretty big even so, a square blue metallic box about eight feet high and perhaps five feet on a side, surmounted by four gigantic red insulators, a weird-looking coil, and a network of cables. These were being hooked up with a portable atomic power-pack of the type that provided power for all purposes on the island.

On its face was a graph indicator, at the top, and a series of controls that governed the action of the huge multi-faceted crystal lens that dominated the front of the panel. In use a heavy shield was fitted over the lens, channelling the powerful radiation emitted from it through a small aperture. The controls were set before operation began and were not thereafter touched until the operation was finished and the fractionator shut down.

The fractionating-rays, so called, could be "tuned" to a particular element, so that they separated the atoms of that element from a volume of sea-water as it passed through the exposed vat, in a kind of "settling" action. This method, made possible by increased control of atomic power and a broader use of the electromagnetic impulses for new effects, had been an enormous improvement over the old-fashioned methods of mineral extraction by evaporation, exchange-resins, or even chromatographic absorption, which was its remote grandfather, allowing as it had for the selective removal of minerals at different points of an absorbing column. The fractionators had made sea-mining really practical on a huge scale.

The technicians were working languidly in the hot-shed, taking great care with the fractionator because if anything went wrong with it they would be the ones who would be right in the front line for destruction. The things were perfectly capable of fractionating people as well as water. But they were not hurrying about it, and they obviously had not heard Kerrick. He decided they were no threat and crept on hip way across the foggy beach.

HE COULD NOT see the dock but he knew it must be ahead of him, and he knew there was a lookout on it, so that he must not make any noise. The shed that held the diving gear was about midway between the test-shed and the dock. He set his feet softly, softly in the wet sand, and a little lapping tendril of water came as warm as blood against his ankles and touched them, and withdrew. Kerrick started wildly.

Then he shook his head and went on. He had been kept too busy the first few days to go looking for Grelvi, and he had believed anyway that the Grelvi would come to the island, make some kind of contact with the intruders if only to warn them away. Instead, every kind of life had been withdrawn from the surrounding seas, as though the island was being isolated preparatory to some uncanny but overwhelming doom.

Something—instinct perhaps, or a process of reasoning too obscure to recognize—told Kerrick that he must not wait any longer, not only for Thane's sake but far his own, and that included the rest of the men an Island 10.

A surface of smooth plastic, greasy with damp, met his outstretched fingers. This would be the shed. He followed the wall with his hand, around the corner and on until he felt the edge of a door. He opened it silently, and stepped inside, pulling it to behind him.

The shed had no windows to leak out a betraying glow. He snapped on a tiny pocket-torch and began to collect and check his gear with nervous haste. He wanted to get going before his nerve ran out.

He had it all stacked together when the door opened and

Truby came in.

"I had a hunch I'd find you here," he said, giving Kerrick a tight-faced, angry look.

Kerrick damned him, "I thought you were asleep."

"I woke up. Okay, Kerrick, tell me. What the hell are you up to?"

"I'll tell you when I get back."

"You'll tell me right now. You've been acting funny ever since we, got here, like you had something on your mind, and I guess you have. You know what Canforra told me this evening?"

"No," said Kerrick, shifting his weight and sweating, "What?"

"He said for me to keep an eye on you. He said he got word straight from Welker, by a guy that came in on the barges today."

"Didn't he give you orders to cut my oxygen-tube or put lead weights in my sample-pouch?" asked Kerrick bitterly.

Truby looked uncomfortable, "No he didn't. And I'll tell you, Kerrick, I don't feel good about the whole thing. I like you personally. But, I can't dive with a guy I don't trust, and the way things are looking it may not be just me, it's all the guys in camp."

"That's just it. Listen, Truby, I have to go out there and try—"

"Try what?" asked Truby. "To save your own skin while the rest of us get slaughtered? You're Thane's pal, he'd take care of you. Maybe you're even—hey! Of course that's it." Truby's eyes blazed. "You're carrying a message from him to his stinking little pets out there."

"Suppose I am," said Kerrick quietly. "I thought everybody was convinced the Grelvi weren't important even if they existed."

"It looks like we were wrong," Truby said, moving

imperceptibly backward toward the door. "I talked to this guy myself. He brought in a load of guns with him—it'll be all over camp tomorrow, you can't keep a thing like that quiet for long. He said—"

"What did he say?" asked Kerrick, moving a little forward, his hands loose and swinging at his sides.

Truby's gaze flicked uneasily from him to the door, measuring distance.

"He said when Welker got Canforra's report he spoke to the Lawmaker, and the Lawmaker spoke to Thane—he's in the fortress, or did you know that?—and Thane said the Grelvi were giving us a warning to clear out and if we didn't—"

He whirled and jumped for the door, and Kerrick jumped after him.

He caught Truby around the waist and they fell together through the door and as they went down Truby yelled with all the piercing power of his lungs.

Kerrick pounded him fiercely, "Shut up," he snarled. "Shut up, you fool, don't you know I'm the only chance you have of living?" But it was too late. There was a shout from the dock and more shouting from the test-shed. Truby thrashed around, fighting furiously. His feet drummed into Kerrick's middle, his hands punched and clawed and hung on. Kerrick had no time for the niceties. He liked Truby, but not enough to die to save him a headache. He pulled the weighted cord Thane had given him out of his tunic and rapped Truby over the crown with it, and Truby became quiet.

Kerrick pulled him into the shed, grabbed up the stack of gear in his arms, being desperately careful to leave nothing behind, and snapped off the little torch.

Then he listened.

The fog had distorted Truby's cry somewhat. There were

a number of people moving about with lights and shouting to one another, trying to find where that cry had come from, Kerrick frowned, breathing heavily. Then he slipped out, carrying the gear, and closed the shed door. Moving with enormous care, he headed hack toward the test-shed, keeping close to the water and watching the erratic gleaming of lights in the thick mist.

AMONG THE TANGLED mess of machinery and material attendant upon the construction of a permanent pumping station beyond the temporary erection at the far end of the shed, Kerrick thought he might find a shelter long enough to get into his diving outfit. He had to get off the island now whether he wanted to or not. Welker had warned Canforra about him, and when Truby came to and talked they would be sure he was carrying a message from Thane to the Grelvi—which he was, but he didn't think they would believe him when he explained what the message was. He thought that, as nervous as they were now and bad as things were beginning to look, they might very probably kill him right on the spot.

He thought that that would be a very nice clean way for Welker to get rid of him, if he wanted to. And he also thought that if Welker was sending guns to Island 10 he must be getting really worried.

And if Welker had become suddenly really worried about the Grelvi, animals or not, Thane's warning must have been impressive. Kerrick thought that things were probably worse back on the main island than even Truby's "guy" was telling.

Could even the power of Thane's name hold these mysterious creatures in check now?

Whether it would or not, he had to try, Otherwise a lot of good men like Truby would die, who were not to blame for any of it.

He had almost reached the test-shed, and almost decided he was safe, when he saw a light on the beach ahead of him, between the shed and the sea, and in the same instant a voice cried out behind him that Truby had been found and some of the gear was missing.

"—diver!" came the muffled cry, full of urgency, "Don't let him get away!"

And the word *Grelvi* echoed mistily from light to bobbing light, and the voices were full of fear.

Kerrick checked and turned, thinking perhaps he could slip past the test-shed on the landward side. But there were lights there, too, moving toward him, and somebody yelled, "There he is! There he is, stop him!"

The open door of the shed was close by, throwing a beam of light into the fog. The long room inside looked to be empty. Kerrick ran into it.

Feet pounded. Voices clamored. Kerrick went leaping down the long room past the vat installations, toward the looming bulk of the fractionator. He had a start on the men behind him and he might have made it out the other end of the shed. But a man came in through another door just beyond the fractionator and sprang at him, swinging a length of pipe like a club.

Kerrick dropped his bundle and grabbed the pipe with both hands as it whistled toward his head. He shortened his grip on it, wrestling the man around, almost banging into the naked lens of the fractionator. Now he could see the others running down the shed toward them. A high harsh voice was screaming insistently, "Kill him! He was going to bring the Grelvi down on us!" The men ran as excited and wild as a pack of young hounds.

The man on the other end of the pipe wrenched frantically to free it. His eyes bulged with fear and rage. "You're in with the Grelvi," he panted. "Trying to kill us all—"

Kerrick hit him desperately on the jaw, snapping his head back. His grip loosened a little on the pipe. Kerrick planted a foot in his belly and pushed. Out of the corner of his eye he saw someone dart in behind the fractionator. The high harsh voice was still screaming, but now it said, "I'll get the bastard! Look out, I'll get him—" The man let go of the pipe and staggered back and Kerrick flung the pipe over his head at the men beyond him, who had now stopped. The pipe was still in the air, the man was still staggering back, and Kerrick was still in the act of turning when it happened.

There was a hum of power as someone opened the master switch. The unshielded lens of the fractionator flared into sudden savage color, yellow and orange like a great evil jewel. A stream of radiation burst from it.

Kerrick was almost directly in front of the fractionator. The man he had pushed away was already past the lens, on one side of it. The radiation should have hit Kerrick full on and left the other man untouched. But the multi-faceted lens was still not coordinated with the series of focusing mirrors behind it. The burst of radiation was directed obliquely to one side instead of to the front. In the space of a second or less it caught the man and stripped the soft substances of flesh and blood away from the bones above his waist, so that for an instant he stood there as a dreadful half-skeleton mounted on strong normal legs that were still walking. Then the bones began to crumble and the legs collapsed and a terrible cry went up from the men on the other side of the machine.

Sick and stunned, Kerrick fled away out the door through which that unlucky man had come to find his death. Only instinct made him reach down and pick up the bundle of diving gear as he passed it. He could hear the men inside shouting with a heavy sound of horror in their voices. The sounds got fainter. Nobody followed him. Apparently shock had stopped them dead for the moment. Kerrick plunged in among the machines and stacked-up piles of material in the construction area.

When he carne to the water's edge he stripped in a frantic hurry and pulled on the harness with the oxygen-pack and the small battery-powered propulsion unit. The powerful underwater lamp he clipped to the belt of his trunks, and he was careful to secure Thane's weighted cord there too, where he could get at it in a hurry. Then he thrust his feet into the light plastic fins, settled the breathing tube in his mouth, and adjusted the mask.

He was all ready: The sea lay before him, a vast silence, a dark entity wrapped in the purple mist, under a starless, moonless sky.

Somewhere out there, beyond the ever-widening ring of death they had set around the island, the Grelvi waited.

Kerrick shivered once. Then he took the shock-spear in his hand and went quickly into the water.

CHAPTER SIX

THE BOTTOM here was a wide shelving bowl without obstruction. Kerrick swam straight ahead without any light until he was sure he was far enough away from the dock to make shooting inaccurate, in case someone should see the offshore glow through a rift in the fog.

The water was warm and caressing on his shin, and very dark. He hated it. The undersea world was his world and he was as much at home in it as a fish. But now, for the first time in his life, he felt that the sea was something to be hated and feared.

No, not the sea. *This* sea—as alien and different from Earth's blue cold waters as the land was different from his native Ohio.

It was no better when he switched on the belt-lamp. The diffuse globe of light it projected around him dispelled the immediate darkness but it also showed up the withered blackened weed and the dead moss, the utter emptiness of the water in which no living thing moved except himself.

He switched on the propulsion unit and plunged deeper and farther into the dark sea, trailing a plume of silver bubbles behind him.

The smooth bowl-like formation broke up, showing deeper rifts and higher, rougher peaks, until Kerrick was moving along the black slot of a valley between walls of rock that gave back a wet glistening where his light touched them. And everywhere there was the emptiness and dead desolation.

It came to him that this must be the power of the Grelvi that the land-people feared so much. All their livelihood depended on the sea. If the Grelvi could sweep the waters dear of life there would be no fish for the nets, no pasture for the scaly herds, no plants in the sea-fields of the farmers. The land-people would starve and die.

He went on, letting the propulsion unit do most of the work so that he could conserve his own strength and his vital oxygen supply. He did not know how long this mission would take him. He did not even know whether the Grelvi were air-breathers, or how they lived, or how he was going to communicate with them.

Doubtless he would find out—if they let him live that long.

He passed out of the area he had explored with Truby. And now he began to encounter reefs of fantastic shape and coloring, some of them standing up like walls from the ocean floor clear up in to open air above the surface, others guarding little level stretches of sand or merely standing about as castles or weird animals or abstract shapes.

Suddenly, across a line as sharp as if it had been cut with a mower's sickle, there was life again.

The bright strange colors of moss and weed shone back at him in the lamp's glare. The naked reefs were clothed in wavering thickets of purple and bronze and gold. Wide eyes peered at him in luminous amazement, sometimes in scattered pairs and sometimes by the hundreds all at once, and there was a constant flicking and shining of bodies, moving, turning, vanishing. Kerrick went on, threading his way more slowly and carefully now among the tumbled reefs and rocks.

After a while he noticed that while weed and moss were still flourishing richly, the mobile life was gone again.

He cut off the propulsion unit and drifted with the idle current, looking from side to side. He did not see anything and yet he was seized with a strange uneasiness.

Reef and rock and weed, all empty and silent in the dark water.

Kerrick thought that things were moving beyond the circle of his light.

Uneasiness turned rapidly to a cold panic.

He fought it down. There was no escape and he knew it. So instead of doing either of the things he wanted to do, which were to swim madly away or else break for the surface and some scrap of dry land, he forced himself to come down quietly on a stretch of clear sand, balancing upright with finny leapings and bowings like a grotesque ballet dancer. He laid down the electric spear and took Thane's weighted cord from his belt and held it up.

And waited.

There was a rush and a swirl above his head. Swift, powerful, terrifying, and splendid, a great golden shape split the water in a smother of silver bubbles, passe over, and was gone. The turbulence and his own instinctive recoil sent

Kerrick spinning. When he regained his balance he realized that Thane's cord was gone, too.

Once more he stood and waited.

All at once there was light, immensely more powerful than his own. It illuminated the whole area I where he stood, as bright as a little sun.

HE MADE himself breathe slowly and evenly, counting.

One, two. In, out. The weed waved with gentle grace along the edges of the light. His body waved too, giving itself to the massive rhythm of the sea. One, two. In, out. And nothing came, nothing showed itself.

Then he saw them.

There were two of them. There must have been a third one with the light, unless it was resting on a ledge of rock, but two were all that Kerrick saw. They swam toward him through the brilliant water, their bodies all shining gold. They were man-shaped except that their hands and feet were modified for swimming, and except that they must have been fully nine feet tall, slender, sleek, and terribly strong. They were obviously air-breathers, and warm-blooded. They looked at Kerrick with great black luminous eyes, fun of a quick but quite alien intelligence, and Kerrick shuddered a little where he stood, as though something cold had brushed across him.

One of the Grelvi carried Thane's cord in his hand.

Kerrick raised both his own hands to show that they were empty of weapons. The Grelvi carried none either, but he suspected that the metal tubes in their girdles—their only article of clothing outside of their own sleek golden fur—probably included quite good weapons. They would not need to use them on him. They could tear him to pieces easily enough with their long webbed fingers.

They came swiftly one on each side or him and grasped

his arms, and Kerrick's flesh shrank away from that alien contact. Once more panic almost overcame him, but before he could think about it he was rushed up toward the surface at a speed that left him dizzy from the buffeting of the water. They broke in a smother of spray and foam and the Grelvi blew like seals, and then one of them spoke in a great deep voice that boomed on Kerrick's ear like the very voice of the sea itself.

"Why have you come here, bearing Thane's weapon?"

Kerrick got the breather out of his mouth, and answered in the same land-Venusian speech, which was as foreign to his tongue as it was to the Grelvi's.

"He gave me that as a token because it bears his stamp. I bring a message from Thane."

They swirled and bobbed in the purple water, like great golden fish.

"What is the message?"

"Thane is a prisoner in the fortress of the Lawmaker."

The Grelvi stiffened and made a deep sighting of rage and sorrow. They spoke briefly between themselves, in their own language. Then they said to Kerrick.

"Come."

Once more they grasped him and he had barely time to get his mouthpiece back in before they were boiling away with him between them, leaving long streaks of phosphorescence behind them. Theoretically they were swimming on the surface, but they were under it as often as not and no human lung capacity could match theirs unaided any more than Kerrick's human frame could match theirs for speed and strength. He let them tow him, and it was like being carried between two power boats only there was no sound but the rush of water. After a while, in spite of himself, he began to enjoy it.

Presently they rolled high out of the water, filling their

lungs for a long dive. Kerrick caught a last glimpse of the surface, mist-shrouded as always, and then the Grelvi plunged down and down in a slanting rush and there was a light on the bottom of the sea, pale and clear as a drowned star, and the light was low in the face of a great dark wall that filled all the watery horizon—a huge reef, Kerrick thought, and felt his heart pounding with fear and excitement. The Grelvi shot straight for the light and past it into a wide tunnel that had guide-lights set along the way. To Kerrick the lights were no more than a fleeting blur and then the Grelvi surfaced again and they were in a wide circular place of light, so beautiful and strange that Kerrick forgot his fear in looking at it.

The water glowed, as though from sources underneath, a luminous circle only lightly touched with mist. All around it the reef rose like the mighty walls of a castle never dreamed by any man of Earth. The eroded, wind-carved rock took the form of battlements, of turrets and spires too fanciful for any human architect, and all the walls and battlements were pierced with light that shone through windowed galleries and tall arches. There was a sound of laughter and of music, and that too was in no way human.

THE GRELVI SWAM with Kerrick onto a sloping ledge of rock that led up out of the water. They shook themselves and Kerrick removed his mask and breather, kicking off the fins that were ludicrously clumsy on land. They led him up the ledge and through a tall bright doorway into a space that was half a cave and half an anteroom. Against one wall a set of diving gear was already neatly arranged. Thane's, of course. They waited while he shrugged out of his own harness and put it beside the other.

Then they led him along a passage and into a very large cave enlarged still further and shaped by hand, with a long gallery open onto the lagoon. There were a number of Grelvi here, men and women both, talking together with a tense air of excitement, while a tall golden girl sang a song as fierce and lovely as the angry sea, accompanied by a harsh wild piping.

"She sings of old battles," said Kerrick's escort, "and of the new ones which are to be, tomorrow."

In the water the Grelvi were born creatures of the sea, but on land they took on the attributes of men. They wore garments of bright cloth and they adorned themselves with pearl and moonstone and ornaments of sea-ivory. Their women were superb, if one could get used to their oddly inhuman faces, hut Kerrick thought that any Earthman would be frightened to death of these huge golden Junos.

He was. He was frightened of all of them. He felt small and wet and inadequate standing there in his trunks and his naked white skin while they all stared at him and began to rise and come forward, and the singing stopped.

There was a great booming and roaring of Grelvi voices. Kerrick caught Thane's name and then another one that sounded like "Zeehn," repeated several times. More and more Grelvi began to pour in from other entrances until the cave-chamber was packed with crowding nine-foot bodies, in all shades of gold from near-white to red-tawny, all looking down with their black strange eyes at Kerrick.

One of his escort bent and said, "You will speak to Zeehn, who is chief among us."

He thrust Kerrick ahead of him along another passage and the whole crowd followed.

The passage ended in a mammoth chamber that must have taken the full width of the reef. The veined greenish-black stone of the walls had been polished to a mirror-like smoothness and inlaid in regular panels with symbols of hammered gold, so that the place had a look of sombre splendor. At one end a huge coiling figure that Kerrick took to be symbolic of the ocean was carved in high relief, stretching great arms as though to embrace and protect. Between those arms was a slab of stone-royal table and altar all in one, Kerrick thought, and obviously very ancient. In the middle of the table, built of bright pebbles, was a pretty little island with its attendant rocks, surrounded by concentric rings of ash.

Island 10.

Seven Grelvi sat around the table, planning, drawing with their fingers in the ashes, lines of approach and attack. They stopped when Kerrick and the crowd came in and six of them Kerrick glanced at and forgot.

The seventh was Zeehn.

All the Grelvi looked liked kings and queens. Zeehn looked like a god. He was still strong and vigorous but his tawny fur was touched with white and his eyes held a deep wisdom. The word "noble" came into Kerrick's mind. Zeehn was a noble creature indeed, and Kerrick thought that when he set his face toward destruction he would be as noble and as ruthlessly terrible as a typhoon.

There was more talk in the mighty passionate voices of the sea-folk. Zeehn listened brooding hugely above the little pebble island that represented the lives of a hundred and twenty-four men, looking hard at Kerrick. When the talk was done he said, "Speak."

Kerrick spoke. His voice sounded thin and ridiculous in his ears after the organ-tones of the Grelvi.

"And that was all the message," he finished. " 'Tell the Grelvi where I am.' Now I've told you. And now I have a message of my own."

One of the councillors started to speak but Zeehn raised his hand.

"Say it, Earthman."

Kerrick pointed to the little island, isolated in its ashen

rings.

"The men of Island 10 are men like me. They are not responsible for the violation of your boundaries, and it will, gain you nothing if you kill them."

There was a rumbling mutter as Grelvi who understood the land-speech translated for those who did not.

Slowly, Zeehn shook his massive golden head.

"They are intruders. They must die. As you would die instantly, if you were not Thane's messenger. As you may still die."

"Well," said Kerrick, "and what of Thane? What would he say to your attack on Island 10?"

"Thane is our friend and brother. He is one of us. But he is not our chief, he does not make our decisions. We will destroy the island at dusk tomorrow if your people have not left by then."

"And," said Kerrick, "before the night is over, your friend and brother Thane will die."

HIS HEART was beating wildly and his voice threatened to show a betraying quaver, but he glared up as haughtily as he could into the eyes of Zeehn.

Zeehn bent forward, "How and why?"

"The Lawmaker is holding him as hostage for your actions," Kerrick said. He did not know that this was true, but it was perfectly possible, and even if it was not true now it might well be later, in the sense that a panicky people might well kill Thane in reprisal for any Grelvi attack. Anyway, it was the only weapon he had and he used it.

"If you strike Island 10, you kill Thane and you don't even touch your real enemies, who are the Lawmaker and the Earthman Welker. Those two between them will keep on until they devour you as they are devouring their own people—unless you fight them with wisdom and cunning as well as courage."

Several of the councillors and a large number of the Grelvi now roared at Zeehn, advising him to kill this creature at once and get on with the attack.

"He only wishes to save his comrades!"

"Which is more than you seem to want to do!" he said heatedly. "Thane went in to the Lawmaker to fight for your rights and because of that he's a prisoner, and yet you care so little for your 'brother' that you won't even think about saving him."

Kerrick was working up a fine head of steam, not only for Thane and Island 10 but for himself.

"If you're so anxious to fight, why not strike at the head where it'll do some good, instead of at an isolated island? How long has it been since you Grelvi have gone outside your reefs?"

That question took Zeehn by surprise.

"Not since the boundaries were set."

"A lot has happened since then. Didn't Thane tell you?"

"He has told us many things," said Zeehn. "Of worlds beyond this one—many things. Our wise men have put them into books. They are of great interest, but they do not affect our lives."

"Oh yes they do," said Kerrick. "The chief men on those other worlds have made laws which protect you from just exactly what's happening to you now. The heads of the Company—Welker's chiefs—are far away on Earth, but they control him. They could stop him instantly from invading your land, on Island 10 or anywhere else. And if they refuse to listen, there are powers above them that will *make* them listen. All it requires is some proof of your ancient claim to these seas, and one message across space to Earth."

"Proof we have," said Zeehn quietly. "What is your plan?"

"Get Thane safely out of the fortress and then join with the land-people, whose cause is much the same as yours, to force the Lawmaker and the rest of the Sulvini to make new treaties and honor them. And I will send a message through to Earth."

He could do that, if once the Grelvi and the ordinary folk of the land—Donavel's party—were in power. The Lawmaker and his guards would no longer be able to censor and control all communication to the outside. And what he had told Zeehn about the laws was true. The Interplanetary Code required that all activities be carried on under strict legal regulation and with the full consent of the native peoples involved.

Welker and the Lawmaker were getting by with it because the Lawmaker claimed Island 10 and therefore the right to lease it. Once the Grelvi came forward the whole business would be investigated, and any violation of their rights would bring thunder and lightning on the heads of those responsible. Especially Welker. And Kerrick would not be unhappy about that. He was convinced that it was Welker's man, back there on the island, who had thrown the switch on the fractionator.

He waited for an answer.

There was a second roar of protest, perhaps not quite so loud as the first. Someone cried, "How can we trust this alien that he is not lying to leading us into a trap?"

Zeehn's wise strange eyes lit with a very cold light. "We have his life as a guarantee."

He reached out one massive hand and scattered, the pebbles of the tiny island on the table. Then he rose.

"We will rescue Thane. It will be as it was in the old time, when our fathers made the Sulvini tremble. After that, we will see. The Earthman's way may prove good. And in any case, there is always time for killing."

An hour later they were on their way.

CHAPTER SEVEN

THE TIME that followed was, to Kerrick, a dizzy mixture of nightmare and wild, glorious dream.

He swam with the Grelvi. Their line was flung out in two long slanting wings, a wedge with Zeehn at the apex, the point of honor. They clove the midnight ocean like the point of a mighty spear, leaving behind them a wake of burning phosphorescence and a trembling in the weed. The same two men that had brought Kerrick to the reef-city had charge of him again, and they kept him close behind Zeehn.

At dawn, when the splintered sunlight was sifting downward through the layers of cloud like a rain of soft fire, the Grelvi raised an island with shelving beaches and shallow bays choked with many-colored weed. And here the line was broken, some of the Grelvi remaining in the water, strung out in a broad half-circle, while others raced on to the island.

The men who were with Kerrick quivered with excitement as they waited, very quiet in the water. One of them whispered, "Watch now—and be ready—"

Flights of queer piscene birds rose flashing from the weed as the Grelvi came. And then all along the beaches there was a stirring, and a grunting and bellowing, and Kerrick saw great bodies moving on the sand and realized that this way a rookery of the Venusian sea-elephant, amphibians half as big as whales.

"Watch now," whispered the Grelvi next to him. "Here, take this, and stay close by us."

He put one of the small metal tubes the Grelvi all carried into Kerrick's hand and showed him how to press a notched trigger—one place for light, two places to stun, three to kill.

Kerrick remembered the oil-wood torches they still used on land and thought it was about time the Grelvi came out of their reefs and shared some of their knowledge.

The roaring and bellowing of the huge beasts on the island rose to a crescendo of alarm. Suddenly at both ends of the long curving beach the golden Grelvi emerged from the weed onto the land and ran swiftly behind the herd, shouting in harsh peculiar cries.

The man next to Kerrick laughed. "They hear," he said, "and understand, but they do not like to obey. They are lazy, the big ones."

The big ones began to move in a long reluctant ragged line, shuffling ponderously down the sand toward the water.

The Grelvi ran among them, shouting, slapping their colossal gray flanks.

The ponderous shuffle quickened, became a lunging, a clumsy gallop. The Grelvi voices rose like bugles above the heavy bellowing. The huge bodies began to hit the water, lashing geysers of spray, tearing out into the weed. Fifty, a hundred, two hundred—Kerrick could no longer see the beach and the shallow hay was a roiling smother of spume and there was a sound of thunder in the sea.

The herd came out of the bay.

"Now!" screamed the man next to Kerrick. "Keep them from spreading—*hai!*"

A huge gray face appeared out of the smother, wild-eyed, with an indignant gaping mouth. The man yelled to Kerrick again but Kerrick could not hear what he was saying and now all the water was full of enormous heads and huge bodies rolling. He saw lights flicker and flash all down the line and he flashed his and some of the creatures blinked and recoiled but others were more stubborn. The powerful Grelvi were darting among the flanks of the herd, in great enjoyment, laying about them with their hands and shouting. Kerrick did not think he was big enough or fast enough for that kind of work. A thoroughly angry bull came churning at him, looming up as big as a mountain, determined to break through the line. Kerrick notched the trigger up to the second position and aimed the now-invisible beam squarely at the creature's massive frontal bone.

The bull gave a kind of grunt, rolled half over and lay still for a moment and then swam slowly back into the herd.

The Grelvi from the beach had rejoined the others, and the herd was held together and driven out to sea.

ALL THAT DAY the Grelvi drove the colossal beasts, and in the afternoon they came upon the floating camp of the ordinary sea-herders from the mainland. The men fell down prone on their raft and covered their faces while the Grelvi passed.

They swept on, toward the fortress island.

They passed sea farmers tending their floating fields of edible weed, and the mighty herd scattered the fields, and the farmers fled in their tiny boats out to sea, wanting no part of what was about to happen to the island.

They passed a fishing fleet, and the fishermen fled too. And Zeehn said to Kerrick, "They are all far out from their former grounds. Is this the Earthmen's doing?"

Kerrick said, "I'm afraid so."

They avoided the little islands where the sea-mining installations were. The Grelvi did not want word to travel ahead of them and they understood that the Earthmen could send it. But they could see even so how the ocean currents were fouled and muddied, how the weed was dying and all the underwater creatures gone.

Zeehn said, "No matter what Thane says, I think we will kill you all. This is an abomination."

Kerrick said, "There's an awful lot of ocean, and I don't

think the land-people would mind if they got something out of it, in schools and hospitals and better ways of living. But the Sulvini take it all and they get nothing."

Zeehn grunted. The herd groaned and protested with mighty bellowings, finding the taste of the water evil. So did the Grelvi find it. But they went on.

Night fell, and there were dim prickings of light ahead in the gathering mist.

A fierce kind of sigh ran through the ranks of the Grelvi and the pace quickened. They drove the herd faster and faster, pricking them on with strange cries that seemed to communicate a sense of urgency to the great beasts so that they began to churn and shoulder through the water as though their lives depended on it. Faster and still faster they went with the, Grelvi behind them, and Kerrick, fighting in the smother of the wake, noticed how subtly the cries of the Grelvi changed until they were communicating not merely urgency but sheer panic to the herd.

And now the speed of their going was such that Kerrick was dazed and blinded by it. His two guardians towed him as before, and when they were high out of the water he could see the vast turmoil of the herd ahead, a welter of foam and huge gray backs rushing like a tidal wave across the sea, and when they were under the surface there was only the dark impact of the water that threatened to tear the breather from his mouth and the harness from his back. But he was not afraid. The motion, the cries, the headlong stampede filled him with a wild excitement.

A shadowy bulk of hill and harbor loomed in the purple night. The lights were bright in the haze. Kerrick made out the two headlands of the harbor, the isolated glare that came from the Jones & Lansing plant, the small craft tossing violently at their moorings as the still water was churned into a maelstrom by the passing herd.

He saw, dimly through the spray, the crowded mass of buildings in the harbor quarter and the black citadel crowning the hill. He wondered if Lella was up there now. He hoped she was. For now the terrible bellowing of the giant sea-herd echoed back from the island; and he thought that beneath that thunderous sound there were thin cries of human panic.

Then they hit the beach.

The ranks of the sea-beasts went first, spreading wide as the Grelvi continued to drive them from behind but let them go forward in any direction they would. Wave on wave of them pounded and thrashed across the sand, onto the quays, into the streets, mad with a fear they did not understand, and the Grelvi would not let them rest.

Kerrick found himself on solid ground. He began to tear off his mask and harness. His guards shook their dripping bodies close beside him and he saw a compact party of ten or more gathering around them and one of them was Zeehn.

"Come," said Zeehn, and Kerrick ran with them, stretching his legs to keep up with them.

And now it was more nightmare than dream.

All along the quays the torches were out, torn down and trampled under huge frantic bodies. Windows and doors were smashed in, the Watching God of the sea-wall was overturned, beached craft were obliterated. And still the Grelvi drove the herd bellowing through the streets, and on all the rooftops people screamed and wept and cried for mercy to the golden lords of the sea.

Kerrick ran with Zeehn and his party.

THEY PASSED through a market place, wrecked and shattered in the wake of the stampede, and burst up out of the steepening streets into the gardens of the Sulvini. And now the herd was tiring, and the soldiers of the Lawmaker came down from the citadel.

"Drive them! Drive them!" Zeehn roared, and the Grelvi drove the huge beasts on through the dark gardens, among the rocking trees. The soldiers had lances and slings and a few guns, which they had from the Earthmen. The indolent tyranny under which these people had lived so long had not encouraged advances in military science any more than it had encouraged peaceful learning, and the Sulvini preferred to keep even its own soldiery from becoming too strong. And now Kerrick understood fully why the Grelvi had used the herd.

The guns killed sometimes, but more often only wounded, and lance and sling merely stung the huge creatures to homicidal fury. Suddenly they did not need to be driven. They saw an enemy, something they could attack and punish. They lunged forward, their roarings rising to a kind of whistling scream. They went into and through the ranks of the soldiers, scattered them, ground them under, smashed them, and sent the remnants flying back toward the fortress gate.

The Grelvi raced through and between the sea-creatures now, leaving them behind. They ran faster than the soldiers easily, without even stretching themselves, golden shadows in the blue night. They caught up with the soldiers and used the stunning beams on them, heaping them in windows before the gate.

"Through the gate!" cried Zeehn, and fifty, sixty, a hundred golden giants poured into the fortress, taking Kerrick with them.

There were still soldiers in the fortress. Lances and slung stones came at them out of shadowed doorways and colonnades that were only long lines of slotted blackness under the torches. Some of the Grelvi cried out and a few of them fell, but they did not stop. Kerrick panted in their midst across courtyards of ancient stone slimy with moss and up a broad stairway, flashing their own weapons as they went—and they were using the third notch on them now. When the pale flickering beams hit a man he fell and did not move again.

There was a pocket of fierce resistance at the head of the great stair. Kerrick fought side by side with the Grelvi to break it, using the weapon they had given him but contenting himself with the stun-ray. A stone struck him an agonizing blow in the lower ribs and a lance just grazed him. Then the fortress soldiers defeated as much by their ancient fear of the Grelvi as by their superior weapons, broke and ran and there was no more fighting.

Zeehn and his party passed swiftly on into the Lawmaker's hall. But Kerrick went no farther than the door.

A number of the Sulvini had gathered in the hall, both men and women. They had obviously left their villas in great haste to take refuge in the fortress. They were standing in an unhappy crowd, the women inclined to be hysterical, the men too paunchy and bewildered to do much of anything.

Sitting on his high seat at the end of the hall was the Lawmaker. Kerrick had never actually seen him before, but he had formed a mental picture of the man and that had not been too far from being accurate. The Lawmaker was a large and impressive man in a magnificent robe, and he wore his cap of office like the crown for which it was a substitute. He looked proud and defiant, ready to face the Grelvi. But underneath the impressiveness was soft fat, and underneath the pride was selfishness and greed, and underneath the defiance was fear.

Zeehn stepped forward. And there was a truly kingly figure, Kerrick thought, and looked urgently for Lella, and did not see her.

The Lawmaker spoke, "By what right do you break the peace and invade my land?"

Zeehn's great voice filled the hall. "By what right do you give my land to the Earthmen?" He moved forward, again, and the Sulvini flinched away from him. "Have you forgotten the ivory tablets that set the boundary-rights of sea and land for all time? They have not crumbled away."

The Lawmaker said, "I will not discuss treaties with you while you remain in my city. Have your men return to the sea, taking their beasts with them and then we will see how matters stand."

Zeehn made a sound in his massive chest. It was not quite a laugh. "We have taken great trouble to come here. We shall stay until our business is done."

"You will go," said the Lawmaker, and now there was just the hint of hysteria in his voice. "You will have everyone of your brutes out of the city within one hour, or Thane will die." He stood up. "Do you understand that? I have him where you won't find him if you take the fortress apart stone by stone, and in one hour he will die unless I personally take the word to spare him."

Kerrick glanced at his two guardians and nodded. They slipped aside from the doorway "Bring a couple more," he said, "and let's go."

"Where?" asked the Grelvi suspiciously.

"To find the women's quarters. The Lawmaker's daughter is our friend—Thane's friend. She'll know where he is."

HE SET OFF along the corridor, and the four tall Grelvi followed. They went through the halls like a whirlwind, opening doors, and on the third level they found one that was barred and the Grelvi broke it open.

Lella was there, just as beautiful as Kerrick remembered, a vivid living thing among women who were like doughy lumps that wailed and screamed. She started a little at the sight of the Grelvi and then ran forward and gave Kerrick her hands.

"I watched the attack," she said, "I cheered you, until my father had me locked up in here. I'm glad you came back safe from Island 10, *litharni*."

Her face showed the signs of strain. He wanted to ask her a lot of personal questions, but instead he said,

"Your father threatens to kill Thane. Do you know where he has him?"

"He wouldn't," said Lella making a little shocked gesture. "Not really. It's only talk—"

"Perhaps," said Kerrick. "But if I were Thane I'd rather not take the chance. Where is he?"

"In the hidden cells. Donavel and Verilan are there too—" She snatched up a long silken cloak and said, "Come on."

Instead of going down as Kerrick had expected, she led them up a winding stair in one of the towers.

"It's a dreadful place just under the roof, with no room to stand upright except for the guard, and only tiny slits for light and air. Father put Thane and the others up here the minute you hit the beach." She handed Kerrick the cloak, "Cover yourself with that, head and all. Have your weapon ready— you will have to be fast. And your friends must stay back out of sight. Now!"

Kerrick padded silently after her up the last wind of the stair. The Grelvi stayed behind.

The stair ended in a round bare room, quite low, with slitted windows, and no furniture except a stone bench where a man might sit and keep watch over the city. Any searcher would have given it one swift look and gone away again. But Lella climbed on the stone bench and rapped three times on a slab in the apparently solid ceiling.

Kerrick stood behind her, muffled in the cloak and sweating, the Grelvi weapon in his hand.

Lella called, "Open up—it's Lella, and I have a message from the Lawmaker."

The stone was lifted up, apparently on weights, and a man's face appeared in the opening.

"What is—" he said, and Kerrick hit him with the stun-ray.

A half-minute later the Grelvi were crouched in the ugly little hole overhead, tearing away by main strength the bars that held Thane on one side and Donavel and his son on the other in cages under the slant of the roof. The guard had no keys on him. But he had, a long stabbing spear, which could only have one use in a place like that. Lella looked at it and her face became very white and grim. She took Donavel and his son aside and spoke to them while Thane and the Grelvi went through their own ritual of greeting.

Then Thane turned to Kerrick. "You've done a splendid job for everyone but yourself. There was a killing on Island 10, wasn't there, the night you left?"

"Yes. They were after me, and somebody pulled the switch on a test fractionator but another poor devil got it. How did you know?"

"The Lawmaker is a frightened man and frightened men boast. Welker has said you killed the man because he was trying to stop you from leaving the island. That's the report he sent to the Company."

"Trying to forestall me in case I did come back from the Grelvi with some charges against him." Kerrick's jaw tightened. "Well, I've got a report of my own to send the Company, and with you and Zeehn and Lella to back me up—"

"You'll have a hard time sending any report now," said Thane.

"Why? The communication center here in the city—"

"It was wrecked last night—by Welker's request. So now the only radio is in the plant, and Welker is not such a fat indolent slob as these Sulvini. He was afraid of trouble and he's got the plant so well defended that with the kind of weapons we can muster—even the Grelvi—we don't have a chance in the world of breaking in."

CHAPTER EIGHT

IT WAS MORNING. The city was quiet now from the fortress to the sea. The battle here was over and the work of cleaning up had not yet begun. During the night the herd had floundered wearily back to sea.

There was still fighting going on. This time it was around the Jones & Lansing plant, and this time the vicious sounds of powerful modern guns punctuated the shouts of men and Grelvi. Donavel had left the fortress soon after his release to rouse his own party, and had talked them into a rather uneasy partnership with the tall golden men of the sea. Together they were making a noisy and threatening attack on the plant, but the guns that Welker had provided and the electrified fences were keeping them back.

"He must have been expecting trouble," Kerrick said grimly. "He's got the place set up like a fortress."

He was standing on the beach below the city, out of sight of the plant. Thane was helping him on with his diving-gear.

"The Lawmaker knew he was facing a revolt," Thane said. "He was counting on Welker to help him put it down under pretext of protecting Company property. They had a very handsome deal planned out between them, if it had only worked."

It would not work for the Lawmaker, who had been deposed. But Welker would remain untouched and Island 10 would continue to be a source of trouble, and the charge of murder against Kerrick would stand unless he could manage to get through his own report in such a way that a thorough investigation would have to be made.

And there was only one way to do that.

Or maybe there wasn't even one way.

Kerrick was about to find out.

He nodded toward the sound of the fighting. "Keep them busy watching the fences," he said. "They'll be less likely to notice us."

The sea-mining operations, being fully automatic, would go on anyway, fighting or not. But the more preoccupied the plant personnel was with other things the better for Kerrick's lunatic plan.

Thane nodded. He said, "Good luck."

Kerrick set his mouthpiece and mask in place and plunged into the water where a score of the Grelvi were waiting.

They swam together, mostly under water, to a point opposite the plant and just on the edge of the area marked off with lines of red danger-buoys. Beyond the buoys the water, became muddy and disturbed, flowing in the manner of a colossal riptide except that its direction was toward the shore instead of away from it. It ended in a vast ugly confusion of chopping wavelets and foam, and there, deep under the surface, were the massive double pipes of the intakes.

Part of Kerrick's job as a diver had been the occasional repair work necessary on the intakes. So he knew how they were set up.

He had explained very carefully to the Grelvi how they worked normally in tandem and at half-load, how the great toothed rotors of the clearing mechanisms caught the weed that would otherwise have clogged the intakes and threw it off into lateral passages where other machinery passed it on as waste. He explained how sometimes something was sucked in that was too large and solid for the rotors to handle, and then they jammed and automatic controls shut off all power to that tube, switching the full load to the other one.

And when that happened, a diver was sent down through one of a series of hatches depending on where the obstruction was, to clear it.

The Grelvi had listened with interest, while Kerrick explained these things and then described his plan. They were doubtful—not of the plan or of their ability to carry it out, but of his. And he had said,

"Well, if I come to grief, you can always turn around and go back."

So they were here, at the edge of the muddy race. The Grelvi paused to surface, keeping low in the water, breathing deep.

Then they dived.

Before dawn, the carcass of one of the sea-elephants killed in the fighting had been towed out and sunk here, anchored with ropes and heavy stones to the bottom. Now the ropes were slashed and the Grelvi braced their mighty hacks and thrust the heavily-buoyant hulk forward.

KERRICK FELT the edges of the current begin to tug at him. The carcass lumped along just clear of the bottom like a hideous balloon. It began to move faster, rolling over and over, and the current pulled it in and gripped it and carried it away, and Kerrick was carried too, whirling in a blind smother of mud and weed. He fought against it but the current was greater than any force he had ever imagined. He lost sight of the carcass. He lost the Grelvi. The current rushed and raced and roared him on toward the all-devouring pipes and he was lost and he knew it. And then powerful hands caught him and powerful bodies joined and strained with his own against the current. He caught sight of the carcass again, ahead of him, lifted up by the force of the water and seeming to fly toward the gigantic round mouths open to receive it. It whirled heavily around, hesitating where the current split in two. Then it chose the right-hand stream and passed on into the pipe and out of sight.

Frantically Kerrick motioned to the Grelvi who were holding him. He saw others around him now, riding that dreadful stream. They swung all to the right, following the carcass. And as suddenly as the snapping of a man's fingers the terrible suck of the current stopped. The pumps on No. 2 Intake were stilled.

Moving fast, before the swirl and suck of the more powerful stream that was already beginning to move into No. 1 could catch them, Kerrick and the Grelvi swam into the huge tunnel of the tube.

And now Kerrick was in the lead and he had no time for faltering or mistakes. The Grelvi, even with their lung capacity, could not stay down forever.

He shot forward. The Grelvi lights lit the water for him showed the white plasticon curve of the tube, and then the first of the series of rotors, with the carcass of the sea-elephant jammed securely in it.

He passed the carcass, slipping between the great unmoving blades that gleamed coldly in the light. The Grelvi followed him, and one swam up beside him and made a gesture urging him to hurry.

He sped on, flying between the blades with their sharp steel teeth. And then he saw the marking on the roof of the pipe and shot toward it. For the safety of the diver the hatch controls worked from either side. He laid hold of them and pulled, and a golden-furred hand reached up and helped him.

A minute or two later they were all standing together in the maintenance shed above, the Grelvi shaking themselves and blowing like whales, Kerrick shedding his gear and inwardly thanking heaven for open air.

The yard of the plant was deserted, Kerrick imagined that the men were all at the fences, facing, the very noisy attackers who were carrying on with enormous vigor. Once in a while a gun went off. Kerrick beckoned to the Grelvi and set off at a run toward the main building.

They met one man on the way, hurrying to or from the fight, but he was no trouble. He stopped in mid-stride, staring at the golden giants who had appeared suddenly around a corner, and completely forgetting that he had a gun in his hand. He opened his mouth to yell, and Kerrick hit him with a Grelvi stun-ray and went on.

Fight or not, there was bound to be somebody in the main building. The party split up into four groups, to enter by different doors, according to Kerrick's plan. With five of the Grelvi he made for the entrance nearest to the communications room.

It was a glassite door. He caught a shadow of movement from inside it just in time to shout a warning and fling himself to one side. In the same instant the door was flung open and someone fired through it, the bullets throwing dirt in Kerrick's face as he rolled. One of the Grelvi roared, with such loud anger that Kerrick thought he could not be badly hit. Then the firing stopped.

Welker's voice rang out of the doorway, "Give yourself up, Kerrick, and I'll let your friends go. Otherwise—"

"Otherwise hell," yelled Kerrick. "The Lawmaker tried that kind of bargaining with Thane and it didn't work. We're coming in."

He was behind some ornamental bushes, part of the planting around the main building. They were inadequate cover. He did not at all want to kill Welker—he was going to need him for the investigation. On the other hand he did not want to get killed himself, and he did not want the Grelvi slaughtered either. Their weapons were too short-range to be effective against guns, and one of the groups that had gone in by other ways would be bound to come upon Welker from inside, any minute now.

HE NOTCHED his weapon carefully to the third position and called softly to the Grelvi to stay where they were. Then he pointed the weapon at a large flowering shrub perhaps ten feet from the door and just inside its range of effectiveness.

"Watch this, Welker," he shouted. "See what the Grelvi, the non-human animals you were so scornful of, can do! This is how they kill the weed so that nothing can live in the sea or on it. This is how they isolated Island 10. This is how they will kill you and every man in the plant. You can't stand against them."

The flowering shrub blackened, withered, drooped, and died.

It took practically no time at all. And Welker watched. At least he did not fire for that moment. Kerrick tried to see into the hall but it was shadowy in there. The lights must have been put out and the sunless Venusian day made all interiors dim. Welker was pressed back against the wall, out of sight, but Kerrick was not looking for Welker anyway, he was looking for the other Grelvi parties.

In desperation he switched the invisible death-beam to another shrub.

"The sea belongs to them, Welker! They control it and you can't steal from them. See?"

The second shrub curled and darkened.

There was a rush of bodies, dim gold in the long dim hall.

Welker cried out.

Kerrick sprang to his feet and ran straight for the door, notching the weapon back to the second position as he went. A shot crashed but no bullet hit him and then he was in the doorway and through it and Welker was standing with his back to him, facing the Grelvi who had come in the back, and one of the Grelvi was falling forward with a slow majesty, a spot of red widening on the bright fur just over his heart.

Kerrick pressed the firing-stud.

Welker gasped as the stun-ray hit him, and then he fell too, but without majesty. Kerrick leaned over him and took the gun out of his hand, and he thought that even in unconsciousness Welker's face reflected the beginning of a tragic realization.

"Tie him carefully," he said to the Grelvi. "Keep him safe."

They did, passing by their dead comrade calmly because this was not the time for mourning.

"And now," said Kerrick, "I don't think there's anything more to stop us from sending that message."

HE SENT IT, while the Grelvi stood guard over the communication room and frightened the young operator into unquestioning obedience. Then he sent word over the Company intercom system to stop the fighting, and the thoroughly bewildered men were ready to obey. In the next hour a truce was patched up, Welker was taken to the fortress and lodged in a safe place, and a ship was sent out to bring the men back from Island 10.

Toward evening Kerrick sat in the great hall of the fortress, talking to Lella and Thane and Donavel. The high seat was empty. The Lawmaker was temporarily a prisoner in his own apartments and would stay so until he had answered the questions of the interplanetary board of inquiry that was already on its way.

"No harm will come to him," Donavel had promised Lella, "but only for your sake. He was an evil ruler."

"And an evil father, too," said Lella. "Nevertheless he is my father, and so I must protect him. Who will they choose in his place?"

Thane grinned. "Who but Donavel? So we see the beginning of another cycle. The hardy herdsmen and fisherfolk replace the Sulvini and become Sulvini themselves."

Donavel shook his head, "Never."

"Ask your grandchildren," said Thane. "You can't fight it. It's the way of the world."

"Oh, stop," said Lella. "Let him enjoy his triumph." She put her hand on Kerrick's arm, "And what of you?"

"I'll be all right," he said, feeling good, feeling happy with her hand touching him. "Some of the Grelvi went along to Island 10. They'll find the man Welker sent out there—the man who actually did the killing—they have a talent for things like that. And with the full testimony before the board, backed up by the ivory tablets of the Grelvi, I don't think any of us have to worry about a thing."

"I think," said Lella softly, "that for the first time since I stopped being a child, I'm really happy."

She didn't take her hand away.

Distant and deep, a sound of chanting came through the seaward windows.

"Listen," said Thane. "The Grelvi are going now."

They went and looked out over the roofs of the city to the beach. The Grelvi were gathered there alone in the blue evening, with the wreaths of mist already blowing in gently from the water. On their shoulders they bore nine of their number who would fight no more. Chanting they walked out into the sea, and then swam, out and out; the golden sea-men of the morning-star world, going home.

THE END

If you've enjoyed this book, you will not want to miss these terrific titles...

ARMCHAIR SCI-FI & HORROR DOUBLE NOVELS, $12.95 each

D-11   **PERIL OF THE STARMEN** by Kris Neville
THE STRANGE INVASION by Murray Leinster

D-12   **THE STAR LORD** by Boyd Ellanby
CAPTIVES OF THE FLAME by Samuel R. Delaney

D-13   **MEN OF THE MORNING STAR** by Edmund Hamilton
PLANET FOR PLUNDER by Hal Clement and Sam Merwin, Jr.

D-14   **ICE CITY OF THE GORGON** by Chester S. Geier and Richard S. Shaver
WHEN THE WORLD TOTTERED by Lester Del Rey

D-15   **WORLDS WITHOUT END** by Clifford D. Simak
THE LAVENDER VINE OF DEATH by Don Wilcox

D-16   **SHADOW ON THE MOON** by Joe Gibson
ARMAGEDDON EARTH by Geoff St. Reynard

D-17   **THE GIRL WHO LOVED DEATH** by Paul W. Fairman
SLAVE PLANET by Laurence M. Janifer

D-18   **SECOND CHANCE** by J. F. Bone
MISSION TO A DISTANT STAR by Frank Belknap Long

D-19   **THE SYNDIC** by C. M. Kornbluth
FLIGHT TO FOREVER by Poul Anderson

D-20   **SOMEWHERE I'LL FIND YOU** by Milton Lesser
THE TIME ARMADA by Fox B. Holden

ARMCHAIR SCIENCE FICTION CLASSICS, $12.95 each

C-3   **INTO PLUTONIAN DEPTHS**
by Stanton A. Coblentz

C-4   **CORPUS EARTHLING**
by Louis Charbonneau

C-5   **THE TIME DISSOLVER**
by Jerry Sohl

C-6   **WEST OF THE SUN**
by Edgar Pangborn

ARMCHAIR SCI-FI & HORROR GEMS SERIES, $12.95 each

G-1   **SCIENCE FICTION GEMS, Vol. One**
Isaac Asimov and others

G-2   **HORROR GEMS, Vol. One**
Carl Jacobi and others

If you've enjoyed this book, you will not want to miss these terrific titles…

ARMCHAIR SCI-FI & HORROR DOUBLE NOVELS, $12.95 each

D-1   **THE GALAXY RAIDERS** by William P. McGivern
SPACE STATION #1 by Frank Belknap Long

D-2   **THE PROGRAMMED PEOPLE** by Jack Sharkey
SLAVES OF THE CRYSTAL BRAIN by William Carter Sawtelle

D-3   **YOU'RE ALL ALONE** by Fritz Leiber
THE LIQUID MAN by Bernard C. Gilford

D-4   **CITADEL OF THE STAR LORDS** by Edmund Hamilton
VOYAGE TO ETERNITY by Milton Lesser

D-5   **IRON MEN OF VENUS** by Don Wilcox
THE MAN WITH ABSOLUTE MOTION by Noel Loomis

D-6   **WHO SOWS THE WIND...** by Rog Phillips
THE PUZZLE PLANET by Robert A. W. Lowndes

D-7   **PLANET OF DREAD** by Murray Leinster
TWICE UPON A TIME by Charles L. Fontenay

D-8   **THE TERROR OUT OF SPACE** by Dwight V. Swain
QUEST OF THE GOLDEN APE by Ivar Jorgensen and Adam Chase

D-9   **SECRET OF MARRACOTT DEEP** by Henry Slesar
PAWN OF THE BLACK FLEET by Mark Clifton.

D-10   **BEYOND THE RINGS OF SATURN** by Robert Moore Williams
A MAN OBSESSED by Alan E. Nourse

ARMCHAIR SCIENCE FICTION CLASSICS, $12.95 each

C-1   **THE GREEN MAN**
by Harold M. Sherman

C-2   **A TRACE OF MEMORY**
By Keith Laumer

ARMCHAIR MASTERS OF SCIENCE FICTION SERIES, $16.95 each

M-1   **MASTERS OF SCIENCE FICTION, Vol. One**
Bryce Walton—"Dark of the Moon" and other tales

M-2   **MASTERS OF SCIENCE FICTION, Vol. Two**
Jerome Bixby: "One Way Street" and other tales

ALIEN SPACESHIPS OVER THE EARTH

The alien's mission was grim, purposeful and ultimately scientific in nature. When he spied a giant poacher spacecraft approaching and then hovering over Earth, the alien put his own ship on an immediate intercept course. His purpose...to stop the poachers from despoiling the planet. However, as his ship came within range of Earth's gravitational field he realized he was too late—the poacher was gone! But the alien soon discovered something else— what was this strange race of oxygen-breathing creatures on the surface of the planet? So out of the star gulfs he came, troubled, searching, and with a warning for Earth no one dared ignore. Never would Earth see his like again—or know the reason why…

CAST OF
CHARACTERS

THE AGENT
He was a dedicated member of the Conservation Service whose lonely existence soon found him in the skies over Earth.

HAL PARSONS
He and his wife were on a peaceful little scientific trek into the wilderness—until an alien spacecraft showed up.

CANDACE PARSONS
A beautiful woman, even dressed in outdoor gear. But she was also a scientist who knew how to do more than just pour coffee.

TRUCK MacLAURIE
This big football star wasn't exactly the scientific type, but his youthful impulsiveness almost got him a ride inside a U.F.O.

GENERAL EADES
The official record showed him to be a tough military man when facing threats from Earth—but what about threats from space?

THE POACHERS
No one knew much about them, except that they ravaged distant planets for their natural ores—and their latest target was Earth.

PLANET FOR
PLUNDER

By
HAL CLEMENT and
SAM MERWIN, JR.

ARMCHAIR FICTION
PO Box 4369, Medford, Oregon   97501-0168

*For more information about Armchair Books and products, visit our
website at...*

www.armchairfiction.com

Or email us at...

armchairfiction@yahoo.com

CHAPTER ONE

A CONSERVATION SERVICE vessel is quite fast and maneuverable as craft of that general type go. But there was little likelihood that this one would catch up with its present target. Its pilot knew that. He had known it since the first flicker of current in his detectors had warned him of the poacher's presence. But with the calm determination so characteristic of his race, he made the small course-correction that he hoped would bring him through the target area at action speed.

The correction had to be small. Had the disturbance been far from his present line of flight, he would never have detected it, for his instruments covered only a narrow cone of space ahead of him. Too many pilots in the old days, with full-sphere coverage, had been unable to resist the temptation of trying to loop back to investigate disturbances whose source-areas they had already passed.

At one-third the speed of light, such a reversal of course would have wasted both energy and time. No one could make a reversal in any reasonable period, and certainly no poacher or other lawbreaker was going to wait for the maneuver to be completed.

Even as it was, this pilot's principal hope lay in the possibility that the other vessel would be too preoccupied with its task of looting to detect and react to his approach in time. Detection was only possible if, like his own ship, the poacher carried a single operator. Unfortunately, a freighter was quite likely to have at least two, even on a perfectly legal flight, and the Conservation pilot had known of cases where poaching machines had crews as large as four.

Even the presence of two would render his approach almost certainly useless, since the loading and separating machinery would require only one manipulator, and the full attention of any others could be freed for lookout duty. Nevertheless, he bored on in, analyzing and planning as he traveled.

Planet for Plunder

The poacher was big—as big as any he had ever viewed. It must have had a net load capacity of something like a half billion tons—enough to clean the concentrates off a fair-sized planet, particularly if it also boasted adequate stripping and refining apparatus. There was no way of making certain about this last factor, for no such equipment was drawing power as yet. And that, in a way, was peculiar, for the poacher must have been in his present position for some time.

Had the driving energies of the poacher been in use, the Conservation ship would have detected them long before, and would have experienced less difficulty in making the necessary course-change. With a scant five light-years in which to make the turn, the acceleration needed for the task was rather annoying. Not that it caused the pilot any actual physical discomfort. It was purely an emotional matter. His economy-conditioned mind was appalled by the waste of energy involved.

Four light-years lay behind him when the poacher reacted outrageously. For the barest instant the attacker dared to hope that he might still get within range. Then it became evident that the giant freighter had seen him long before, and had planned its maneuver with perfect knowledge of his limitations.

It began to accelerate almost toward him, at an angle that would bring it safely past. It would sweep past just out of extreme range if he kept on his present course—and probably well beyond trustworthy shooting distance, if he tried to intercept it. For an instant, the agent was tempted. But before a single relay had clicked in his own small craft he remembered what the poacher must already have known— that the planet, which had perhaps already been robbed, came first.

It must be checked for damage, even though it was uninhabited as far as anyone knew. The mere fact that the poacher had stopped there meant that it must have something worth taking. It must, therefore, be tied as soon as possible into the production network whose completeness and perfection was the only barrier between the agent's race and galaxy-wide starvation.

He held his course, therefore, and broadcast a general warning as he went. He gave the thief's specifications, its course—as of the last possible observation—plus the fact that it seemed to be traveling empty. The absence of cargo was an encouraging sign. Perhaps no damage had been done to the world ahead. Unfortunately, it might also mean that the raider had a higher power-to-mass ratio than any freighter the agent had ever seen or heard of. But that he seriously doubted. He assumed that the ship was without cargo, and worded his warning accordingly.

His temper was not improved by an incident that occurred just before the giant vessel passed beyond detection range. A beam, quite evidently transmitted from the fleeing mass of metal, struck his antenna, and the phrase, "Now, don't you just hope they'll get us!" came clearly along the instrument.

Again, relays almost closed on the Conservation flier, but the agent contented himself with repeating his warning broadcast and adding to it the data that had inevitably come along with the poacher's taunt—data concerning the personal voice of the speaker. Then he turned his attention to the problem of the planet ahead.

He would need more energy, of course. The interstellar speed of his craft had to be reduced to the general velocity of the stars in this part of the galaxy, for he could not make the survey that would be needed, merely by viewing the planet as he flashed by. He could, of course, get a pretty good idea of the metals that were present through such flash-technique, but he needed information as to their distribution. If he were lucky—if the poacher had actually failed to load up—there would almost certainly be concentrates worth recording and reporting to Conservation.

The sun involved was obvious enough, since it was the only one within several light years. The agent thought fleetingly of the loneliness, even terror, that would descend upon the average ground-gripper in close proximity to the nearly empty space at the galaxy's rim and timed and directed his deceleration to bring him to rest some twenty-four diameters from the sun's photosphere.

The poacher had begun to travel long before he drew close enough to detect individual planets, and he was faced with the problem of discovering just which planet or planetoid had been visited. There were certainly enough to choose among and he was reasonably sure he had detected them all as he approached.

The possibility that he had been moving directly toward one for the whole time, and had, as a result, failed to observe any apparent motion for it, was too remote to cause him concern, particularly since it turned out that he had been well away from the general orbital plane of the system. He had the planets, then. But which ones were important?

Since he would have to check them all anyway, he didn't worry too much about selection. After using up the energy and time needed to stop in this forlorn speck of a planetary system, it would be senseless to leave anything unexamined. Why, he reasoned, should anyone else have to come back later to do what he had left undone? Still, he thought it would be pleasant to determine quickly what the poacher had accomplished, if anything.

The innermost planet, Mercury, was definitely not the plundered victim. It had plenty of free iron, of course, and the agent noted with satisfaction that the metal was not concentrated at its core. If it ever became necessary to seek iron so far out in the galaxy, stripping it from so small a world would be relatively easy.

However, the important metals seemed to be dissolved and distributed with annoying uniformity through the tiny globe—a fact that was hardly surprising. The planet was too small, and its temperature was too high to permit either water or ammonia to exist in liquid form. The ordinary geological processes that produced ore deposits simply could not function here.

The second world was more hopeful—in fact, it seemed ideal on first survey. There was water, though not in abundance. Nevertheless, in the billions of years since the planet had formed a certain amount of hydrothermal activity had gone on in its crust, and a number of very good copper, silver, and lead concentrations appeared to exist. The agent decided to land and map these after he had completed his preliminary survey of the system. If this was the world the poachers had been sweeping, they had evidently failed to get much. This planet, Venus, might be the plundered planet.

It proved not to be, however. The third planet was Earth. Earth's water is not confined to its lithosphere—it covers three quarters of the planetary surface. It washes mountains into the seas, freezes at the poles and, at high elevations, even at the equator. It finds its way down into the rocks and joins other water molecules that have been there since the crust solidified. It picks up ions, carries them a little way, and trades them for others.

In short, Earth contains enough water to produce geological phenomena. The agent saw this almost in his first glance. He wasted a brief look at the encircling dry satellite, then he turned all of his attention on the primary planet itself. He even began to ease his ship outward from the orbit it had taken up, twenty million miles from Sol.

This, he decided, must be the world of the poacher's selection. Even without analysis, anyone with the rudiments of a geological education would know that there must be metal concentrations here—and a civilization that uses half a trillion tons of copper a year can be expected to have at least a few trained geologists.

The agent pointed the nose of his little cruiser at the tiny disc, shining brightly eighty million miles away. He drove straight toward it, combing its surface as he went with the highest-resolution equipment he could bring to bear. All over the surface, and for a mile below, those radiations probed and returned with their information. The agent swore luridly as the indicators told their tragic story.

There *had* been concentrations, all right. There were still a few. But someone had been scraping busily at the best of them, and had left little that was economically worth recovering. It was the old story. If good deposits and poor ones were worked at the same time, the profit was of course smaller. But at least the deposits lasted longer.

An eternity had passed since any legal operator of the agent's race had worked the other way, stripping the cream for a quick profit and letting the others go. Such a practice would have crippled the industry of the agent's home planet millions of years before, had it not been checked sternly by the formation of the Conservation Board.

Crippled industry, to a race at the stage of development his had attained, was the equivalent of a death sentence. Not one in a thousand of his people could hope to escape death by starvation if the tremendously complex system of commerce were to break down.

The agent knew that—like most of his profession—he had seen border worlds where momentary imperfections in the system had taken their toll.

His fury at the sight of this planet mingled with—and was fed by—the memory of the horrors he had seen. Apparently, he had been wrong. The poachers had gotten away with their load—in fact, scores of them must have been at work.

No one ship, not even the monster he had seen so recently, could have done such a job without assistance on a planet of this size. The Conservation Department had suspected, before now, that it faced a certain degree of organization among the poachers. Here was infuriating evidence that the suspicion was all too well founded.

Thought followed reaction through the agent's reception apparatus and through his mind, before his ship was within a million miles of the planet.

At that range no precise mapping was possible. In a sense, surface mapping was no longer necessary, since the surviving deposits were hardly worth the gathering—but the tectonic charts would have to be obtained as usual.

A world like this was in constant change. A million, or ten, or a hundred million years from now the natural processes within its crust would have brought new concentrations into being. These forces must be charted, so that proper predictions could be obtained. Only through such research and predictions could Conservation beat the poachers to the next crop of metal, when it appeared.

The agent began to decelerate again, now matching his velocity with that of the planet itself. At the same time, he began a more detailed analysis of the surface, refining it constantly as the distance diminished. The water he already knew about. He had supposed the gaseous layer would consist of methane and water vapor, with perhaps some ammonia, formed at the same time as the rest of the planet. But his instruments told a different story.

Earth had lost its primary atmosphere. The tragedy had occurred before the first member of the agent's race had ventured away from his own planetary system. The agent found the free oxygen, and swore again. He knew what that meant—*photosynthesis*. The planet was infected by those carbon compounds that behaved almost like life, except for their ferociously rapid rate of reaction.

They were not very dangerous, of course, but due care had to be exercised, and constant vigilance maintained. A good many planets in the liquid-ammonia-liquid-water temperature range had them, and techniques had long since been worked out for conducting analysis, and even for mining in their presence, destructive as they often were to machinery.

The Conservation vessel, naturally, was constructed of alloys reasonably proof against any attack by free oxygen or the usual run of the carbon compounds. In fact, if this world had any unique developments of the latter the agent could always lift his ship out of the atmosphere. Such a retreat seemed to put a stop to the growth of photosynthetic life.

It never occurred to the agent that concealment might be in order. In the first place, he was on a perfectly legal mission. In the second, equally of course, he didn't think that there might be anyone on the planet to observe his arrival.

Oxygen being what it is, he had automatically classified the world as uninhabited and uninhabitable. As a result, the events of the half-second following his machine's penetration of Earth's ozone layer demanded a rather drastic revision of his outlook.

The radar beams, for an instant, made him suppose that another ship was on this world, and was trying to communicate with him. He had almost begun to answer before he realized that the radiation was not modulated, and could hardly be speech—or, more accurately, that its modulation was too simple and regular to represent words. Even though such radiation did not mean intelligence, however, it obviously did imply the presence of life.

Somehow, an organism must have evolved in an oxygen atmosphere with the ability to reduce metal oxides or sulfides, and keep them reduced to free metal. At the moment, it seemed to be a low order of life. But if it continued to develop as the agent's own species had done, this corner of the galaxy might become rather an interesting place in time. A man might have drawn a somewhat similar conclusion from hearing the chirp of a cricket under analogous circumstances.

At first, the agent supposed the radiation to have meaning similar to that of the cricket's chirp, too—it came and it went, regularly and monotonously, from a seemingly fixed source, and had an apparent willingness to go on until the sun cooled. But, a few milliseconds after the first pulses struck his receptors, others began to come in. They shared the simplicity of pattern shown by the first, but there were more of them.

As the ship moved, and its distance from some of the sources changed, it became evident that the waves were being directed in beams, rather than broadcast in all directions— and that the beams were following the ship. Intelligent or not, *something* was at least aware of his presence.

A score of hypotheses ran through the agent's mind during the next few milliseconds, for thought can move rapidly, when the neurons involved are of metal, and the impulses they carry are electronic currents, rather than potential differences between the surfaces of a colloid membrane. But none of these theories managed to satisfy him.

Even he could not continue to theorize at the moment, for the hull of his vessel was glowing bright red, and the surface of the planet was coming up rather rapidly to meet him. He had to land within the next few seconds, assuming that he did not want to do his theorizing hanging motionless in the atmosphere.

The outer surface of his hull was a trifle hard to manage at its present temperature. But none of the myriads of relays further in had been affected and the sliver of metal obeyed his thoughts as it always had, slowing to a dead halt a few yards above the surface and then settling down for a landing while the agent analyzed the material directly underneath.

It was pure luck that there was no vegetation below him—

luck, at least, for any local fire fighters. The hot walls did respond to control, albeit a trifle sluggishly. Particles of sand and clay, coming in contact with the hull began to dance, like bits of sawdust on a vibrating plate. And like sawdust, the dance carried them into a particular pattern.

The pattern took the form of a hollow under the hull, while the excess soil heaped up around it on all sides. The ship eased gently downward into the crater thus formed, which deepened as it continued to sink. The settling of the vessel, and the deepening of the hole, continued for perhaps twenty feet, before the hull touched solid rock.

When it did, more relays moved, and the rock itself flowed away in fine dust. This continued for only another foot, and then the ship was resting in a perfectly fitting cradle of stone, and the displaced soil was drifting back around it, covering its still red-hot circumference. The sand smoothed itself into a low mound that almost, but not quite, covered the vessel.

Had the agent cared about concealment, of course, he could have dug a little deeper—but all he wanted was good contact with bedrock. There was much mapping to do, and the matter of local life would have to wait until it was done.

CHAPTER TWO

IT WAS ONE of the new, triangular, floating radar installations, some two hundred miles northeast of the Virginia Capes, that first picked up the track of the interstellar visitor. Since the vessel was still well up in the Photosphere, far too high for even the latest model planes, the report was worded, ...*Unidentified Flying Object, altitude (tent.) 50 mi. plus, speed (tent.) 3,600 mph, direction northwest by west...*

The ever-watchful, and supersensitive network, set up to guard the lives and property of a continent, responded with an instant alert. In the central communications hall of a huge building near Washington, D. C., worried experts and officials gathered around plotting boards or stood in tightlipped silence before a gigantic map on which reports were automatically registered in moving beams of light. The International situation was hardly tense enough to make probable an immediate enemy action. But in a Cold War period there could be no let-up of suspicion or instant readiness to act.

"The damned thing, whatever it is, is headed straight for Chicago," growled a gray-haired brigadier general, whose face was seamed and leathery from hundreds of air-combat hours.

"She's coming down, too," replied a civilian expert, frowning at the latest reports, which were coming in with increased rapidity as the strange aerial object swept over thickly populated sections of the country. "Altitude only thirty miles over Akron. And she's losing speed by the minute."

"That's what worries me," replied the brigadier unhappily. "If it were a meteor it would be picking up speed. It would be blazing like a comet, even in broad daylight."

"Nobody has yet developed a long-range missile control that will brake an enemy aircraft over the target," said a third member of the high-echelon group, one who wore the light gray-blue of a naval officer in summer uniform. He spoke quietly, almost shyly, but his chest, beyond a highly colored array of battle and medal-ribbons, carried the heavy silver wings of a command pilot.

"I don't like it," said the brigadier, thrusting his hands deep in his trouser pockets. "Just because we don't have this sort of long-range missile control, doesn't mean that *they* haven't come up with it. All those scientists they've been turning out—and the hotshots they grabbed when they moved into Germany, in nineteen forty-five—" He let it hang there.

"Lord knows, meteors have been known to act freakishly," said the naval air officer.

At this point, Great Lakes Station came in with a report that put the UFO, still slowing, still descending, at a point well west of Chicago. There was a general sigh of relief.

But the brigadier remained unhappy. "We'll have to alert every interceptor group in the Northwest," he said quietly. "At the rate that mystery crate is coming down, we'll be able to track up after it any minute now—shooting."

It was the civilian who voiced the thought that had been in all their minds—the thought which none of the others had dared to put into words. He said, "That's going to do us a hell of a lot of good, if she turns out to be a flying saucer. She'll simply take off and zoom out of range."

Nobody answered him, though long looks were exchanged. Then they all went back to checking reports, to planning the interception that seemed to grow more possible with each passing minute. The path of the object seemed to be turning more directly west as its speed continued to lessen, and its altitude to abate. Interceptor command groups within range of its path were ordered to stand by for scramble. Unfortunately, as the object came within Nike range, it was in a part of the continent where no rocket interceptors had been installed.

Then came a phone call from more than 2,000 miles away—from the lips of the general commanding the nation's Intercontinental Bombing Command. In accordance with their routine of constant test-missions, a squadron of B-52's, much too high for civilian observation, had been carrying out an overnight mock-bombing flight from its home field, in Texas, to a uranium mining complex far up in Northwestern Canada, near Great Slave Lake. Currently, they were making their return journey back to Texas.

Said the commanding general, his voice curiously crisp despite its nasal Midwestern drawl, "Three of my observers just spotted your UFO, flying a course a few points north of due west. It was two miles above them, moving at more than fifteen hundred. It was round and red-hot."

"You mean round—like a saucer?" the brigadier asked, his voice breaking.

"No—it was round like a cannonball. And hotter than an H-bomb!" was the response.

When he hung up, Minneapolis came in. Object safely past, still descending, still losing speed…Bismarck, North Dakota, had the object heading due west. Then came a ground observer report from Miles City, Montana, and another from Billings. In both cases, it had been seen as a round, red-hot object, streaking westward across the sky.

Then, nothing…

It was a rough day for the Radar Network.

IT WAS ALSO, as events were to confirm, a rough day for Field Expedition Seven, Summer of 1957, Montana

University of Mines, Departments of Geology and Climatology.

Measured by its human components the expedition was a modest one and consisted of Assistant Professor Harold Parsons, his wife, Candace, and a Climatology Fellow and Field Worker, Donald MacLaurie, known to the regional sportswriters as *Truck*.

Their equipment consisted of one jeep with a two-wheel trailer, two tents that had just been stowed away for daytime travel, canned food supplies, and an assortment of tools and instruments, including a Geiger counter bootlegged by Truck MacLaurie and currently the subject of argument between Truck and Professor Parsons.

"Listen, Truck," Parsons said, with all the patience he could muster. "This is a university field expedition, not a uranium hunt. If you want the credit you'll need to play football this fall, you'll keep that click-box out of sight and out of mind. We're here in the hills to study variations in surface clues to copper-ore formations—that is, *I* am here for that purpose. With your help, of course—if help is just the proper word for it. Candace is here to study cloud formations in the hills, for long-range precipitation effect on mining operations at Butte and Anaconda. I'm hoping you'll learn enough about geology to enable me to give you that credit come September—without putting a permanent mortgage on my professional integrity."

"Golly, Doc—I only intended to try her out during my spare time," protested Truck.

"What I'm trying to say, Truck, is this....there isn't going to be any spare time on this trip." Parsons paused, and added with a trace of acid, "You're not back sleeping in classroom now. You're in the field.

Parsons didn't have to look at his wife to know how she was reacting to his lecture. Not that Candace would show disapproval in the presence of an outsider. But he was all too familiar with the slight blankness of her usually alert and sympathetic brown eyes, the invisible aura of coolness that surrounded her. There were moments when he wished she wasn't quite so sympathetic and outgoing in her relations with people. It only made his own diffidence more pronounced.

Nor was he helped by the fact that—though he stood a wiry six feet one in his socks—he still had to look upward to meet Truck MacLaurie's large and blandly child-like blue eyes. He also felt hampered by the fact that, while he himself was close to thirty, and Truck a mere twenty-two, the big ox looked about five years his senior.

He was about to cut it short and say, "All right, let's get started," when the UFO passed, whizzing, over their heads.

It could not have been more than a mile above them, and it was round as a gigantic egg from some monster bird, red hot as a cooking stone in some giant's barbecue-pit. It was traveling like a bat out of hell, due west, and it was falling fast. Even at that distance, it left in its wake a lingering sense of tremendous heat.

"Golly!" said Truck, following the object's progress with open disbelief. "It's gonna crash into that hill, head-on!"

The expedition of three had made camp, the night before, close to the center of an arid valley in the eastern foothills of the Rockies, roughly halfway between the mining communities of Brown and Hamilton. And camped there they still were, in a district where even the decaying remnants of ghost mining communities were scarce. It was rough, wild country—about as rough and wild as Rocky Mountain foothill country can ever get.

The western end of the valley was blocked by a range of minor hills whose topmost peak rose no more than five thousand feet from the valley floor. Unerringly, the speeding object appeared headed for this peak. Looking on with a mixture of amazement and disbelief that precluded horror, Parsons tried to remind himself that perspective played strange tricks, and that the object, whatever its nature, was undoubtedly on a course that must carry it hundreds, perhaps thousands, of miles before it crashed into the rugged terrain.

Then, unaccountably, the object swerved to the south, avoiding collision as neatly as a plane skillfully piloted by a crack ace. It disappeared *around* the peak, not *over* it, and vanished from sight behind the ragged mountain wall.

Then, there was nothing...no crash, no explosion. Nothing at all.

"Hal honey," said Candace Parsons, "will you, for the love of Osiris or whatever gods you worship, light me a cigarette?"

Not another word was spoken for almost two minutes. The three of them stood there, spellbound, staring at the wall of hills, waiting for something, for anything. But there was nothing.

Again, it was Candace Parsons who broke the silence. She was a trim, long-legged girl, with soft brown hair with a texture so fine that it defied shop and home permanents alike. She was remarkable, too, in that her figure and appearance remained pleasantly female, despite her all-over ranginess and the disfigurement of camping clothes.

She said, "Since neither of you geniuses has any idea of what it is, I think we ought to report it, don't you?"

Parsons nodded. He stepped on his own cigarette and ground it out in the sandy soil. "Perhaps if that damned transmitter of ours can clear those hills we came through yesterday..." He let the sentence trail off, and with Truck MacLaurie went back to the jeep.

The two of them broke the radio out of the trailer and set it up in the open. After fifteen minutes, it became clear that they were not going to get through. Parsons disconnected the transmitter and nodded to Truck to cease winding the battery. He looked at the football player almost pleadingly.

"No, Doc," said Truck. "If you think I'm gonna wheel this buggy back over the hills while you and Candace have all the fun... Well, the answer is no. Let the credits fall where they will."

"Why, Truck—" exclaimed Candace, who had taken a Bachelor of Arts degree in English at a Midwestern university one year before her interests had veered to Parsons and climatology. "That's almost poetic."

She saw the way both men were looking at her and shook her head. "I'm not going back either," she added firmly. "I've always wanted to look at a UFO, and if you think I'm passing up this chance—"

Parsons squinted at the hills ahead. He said, "Okay, mutineers. Let's get this show on the road. We can run up the transmitter when we hit the next range of hills, and maybe get a message through to Hamilton or Stevensville."

A moment later, as they took their places in the jeep, he asked: "Candace, you wouldn't kid me, would you?"

"Who's kidding?" she countered. "That thing didn't look like a flying saucer, but it didn't look man-made either. And who ever heard of a meteor with sense enough to detour *around* a mountaintop?"

"Maybe it's a good thing I brought the click-box along after all," said Truck, who was massively filling the rear seat of the jeep. "You can't tell what that thing may be radiating when we find it."

"*If* we find it," Parsons said quietly, steering the rugged little vehicle neatly around a treacherous rock outcropping that lay concealed by a mask of brush.

The object, whatever it was, had flashed over the valley in less than a minute, covering the same distance by ground that had taken the expedition almost all day.

Throughout the morning, and early afternoon, the hot summer sun beat unmercifully down upon them out of a pale blue sky, reddening already painful sunburns and causing Truck MacLaurie to break out with a rash of prickly heat that had him scratching himself almost continually.

They made only a brief stop for lunch—under a low hill that offered a very poor kind of shade. They would not have stopped at all, but Candace insisted they needed to stretch their legs even if they had lost their appetites. She served them slices of processed ham on crackers, and coffee so hot that Truck wanted to know whether she had actually used the heater or had merely left it out in the sun for two or three minutes.

When they resumed their journey, they found the sun shaded by freshly assembled clouds, which caused the big football player to mutter, "Thank God! We've got the weather on our side, anyway."

"I don't like it," said Candace, staring thoughtfully at the western sky ahead. The jeep was bumping its way up toward the mountains, and something in her tone caused Hal Parsons to slow down and look at her sharply.

"What is it, baby?' he asked.

"According to meteorological tables, there has been an average of only one inch of rainfall in these hills during August," she said. "Furthermore, there has never been a *single* rainfall of more than a quarter of an inch. Those clouds piling up ahead spell out heavy rain to me."

"Speaks the climatologist," said Parsons, concentrating on a barren, rocky patch of hillside ahead.

"Speaks a girl who'd like to know what's going on," Candace replied.

In the rear seat, Truck MacLaurie scratched, sweated and said nothing.

Slowly, circuitously, Parsons and Truck got the little jeep and its trailer up the road-less hillside, and set its course toward a notch in the hills ahead. It was after five o'clock when they reached the summit of the pass and could look down into the valley on the other side of the range. To all intents and purposes, it was an exact replica of the valley from which they had so painfully emerged.

"I don't see anything," said Truck, letting his eyes roam the panorama of scrub and sand and eroded rock that stretched out before them.

"I don't either," said Parsons, battling a feeling of disappointment that he knew to be absurd. There was no reason to believe that a flying object capable of detouring the mountain peak on their right would have selected such a barren piece of earth as its resting-place. It could just as easily have steered past other peaks, over other valleys, until it reached a wide, fertile valley.

"Look at those clouds!" said Candace Parsons, staring not

at the valley or the range of hills opposite, but at the sky above. "If we don't get ourselves set up quick, we'll be in for a serious wetting."

"Hello!" Parsons exclaimed, following his wife's gaze. "It does look grim—and it seems to be right overhead. Come on, Truck."

"I'm glad we're up here, instead of down there," said the king-sized young gladiator, moving to help his professor with the camping gear. "Only time I ever saw clouds like that was in Colorado, when I played left guard for a junior college. We wound up with a flash flood that wiped out half the campus. I came up to Montana Mines the next year."

"Better give the radio another chance, before you break out the tents, Hal honey," Candace Parsons suggested. "I'll take charge of them until you get a message through."

Even as she spoke, a large drop fell on her forehead, and the slow patter of beginning rain rustled around them. She got busy with the tents, moving swiftly, efficiently, and with surprising strength for a slim-looking woman. But her mind was on the weather that was encompassing them.

It simply couldn't be happening—but it was. Great gray-and-white, swirling masses of cloud had boiled over to fill the heavens above them, and the fall of rain was increasing steadily. Her experience told her that these were not cloudburst formations, from which only a flash flood could be expected. Despite Truck's concern, they looked more like the prelude to long, steady rain. Yet they were low, closing down relentlessly, making the ceiling almost invisible as they blanketed the taller peaks that rimmed the valley.

It was her husband who broke through her abstraction, saying, "Honey, come here. I got through to Stevensville. According to them, every watcher and radar post has been alerted all day. And we're the furthest west observers to have seen that thing. They've only been waiting for another report to start an air search."

"If it landed anywhere around here," said Candace, eyeing a sodden cigarette in disgust, "they won't be able to get a plane over these peaks for quite a while—not even a helicopter."

CHAPTER THREE

THE RADAR BEAMS had stopped—or had, at least, ceased to reach the Conservation Agent—before he had gone underground. The point where he had landed was not in line-of-sight range of any of their stations. Needless to say, however, their operators had not forgotten him.

The agent was not considering possible radar operators. In fact, he would not have considered them even if radar had been, to him, something produced by a machine. He was far too busy listening.

If a human being puts his ear close against a wall, or a doorjamb in a fairly large building, he will pick up a remarkable variety of sounds. He will hear doors closing, windows rattling, and assorted creaks and thuds whose origin is frequently difficult or impossible to determine. The one thing he will not hear is silence.

The crust of a planet is much the same on a vastly greater scale. It is always full of vibrations, ranging from gigantic temblors—as square miles of solid rock slip against similar areas on the two sides of a fault plane—to ghostly echoes of sound and the faintest of thermal oscillations as the sun's heat shifts from one side of a mountain to the other, and the rocks expand and contract to adjust to the new temperatures.

These waves travel, radiating from their point of origin, being refracted and reflected as they enter regions of differing density or elasticity, losing energy as they go by heating infinitesimally the rock through which they pass. They may die out entirely in random motion—heat—while still inside the body of the planet. Or a good, healthy wave train may get all the way to the other side.

If it does so on Earth, it takes about twenty minutes. Then a fair proportion of it bounces from the low-density zone that is the bottom of the atmosphere, or the top of the lithosphere, whichever you prefer, and starts back again.

And every variation in density, or crystal structure, or elasticity, or chemical composition, has some effect on the way such waves travel. They may speed up or slow down. Transverse waves, or the transverse components of complex waves, may damp out (have you ever tried to skip rope with a stream of water?) and the compressional waves alone go through. Transverse waves, polarized in one direction, may be refracted through an interface, where the same sort of wave striking the same interface—at the same angle but polarized differently—may be reflected from it.

The important thing is that constantly varying conditions affect the waves. And that means that the waves carry information.

It is confused, of course. Temblors come from all directions, from all distances, due to many different causes, and through all sorts of rock. Interpreting them is not just a matter of sitting down to listen. One might as well tune in a dozen different radios to as many different musical programs, while sitting in the middle of a battlefield with a thunderstorm going on, and try to decide how many flutes were being used in one of the orchestras. The information is there, but selectivity and analysis are needed.

The agent was equipped for such selectivity, such analysis. His sensitive gear could detect any motion of the rock, down to thermal oscillation of the ions, at frequencies ranging from the highest a silicate group could maintain, to the lowest harmonic of a planet the size of Jupiter.

If his instruments proved inadequate, he could listen himself. But since just listening would involve the projection of a portion of his own body through the hull and bringing it into contact with the rock, the act would put a crippling strain on his stone-like flesh, and would consume several millennia of time. He did not plan to take this alternative. Machines were built to be used. Why not use them?

His own senses reacted at electronic speed—were, in fact, electronic in nature, as were his thought patterns. The process of receiving a group of impulses, and of solving the multiple-parameter equations necessary to deduce all the facts as to their origin and transmission, called for just such a fast-acting computer as his mind, though even he took some time about it.

This, primarily, was because he was careful. A temblor originating nearby would naturally have fewer unknowns worked into its waveform by the time it reached him. Therefore, it represented a simpler problem. Also, when solved, that problem provided quantities that could be fitted directly into the equations for more distant wave-sources, since their wave-trains must have come through the same rocks as they approached him.

His picture of the lithosphere around him grew gradually, therefore, and by concentric shells. He saw the layers of different sorts of rock and, far more important, the stresses playing on each layer—stresses that sometimes damped out to zero in the endless, tiny twitchings of the planet's crust and that sometimes built up until the strength of the rocks, and the vastly greater weight of overlying materials could no longer resist them, and something gave.

He sensed the change, as trapped energy built up the temperature in a confined volume, until the rock could no longer be called solid, even though the pressure kept it from being anything that could be called liquid. He saw the magma pockets formed in this way migrate, up, down, and across in the crust—like monstrous jellyfish in a viscous sea.

He saw certain points on the planet where they had

reached so nearly to the surface that the weight above could no longer restrain the pressure of their dissolved gases. An explosive volcanic eruption is quite a sight, even from underneath.

His senses, through the vessel's instruments, probed down toward the core of the world, where magma pockets were more frequent. In such pockets, held in solutions that might some day carry them to the upper crust, they would be accessible—the copper and silver and molybdenum, and other metals his people needed. They would lay diffused through the material of the planet.

Those were the things that interested him. He needed to know the forces at work down there—not in general, as a climatologist knows why Arizona is dry, but in sufficient detail to be able to pre-diet when and where these metals would reach the upper crust and form ore bodies. The fastest electronic computers man had yet built would be a long time working out such problems, given the data. The agent was certainly no faster, and was less infallible.

He knew this to be so and therefore spent much of his time checking and rechecking each step of the work. The task took all his attention, and, for the time being, he was totally indifferent to impulses originating near the surface— much less to a number of feeble ones that originated above the surface.

There was something a good deal more interesting than human reactions to claim the attention of the Conservation operative. He had, of course, confirmed long since his original impression that the ore beds of the planet had been looted. His principal job now was to decide how long the normal diastrophic and other geological processes would require to replace them.

On a purely general basis, replacement should take tens of

millions of years for a planet of Earth's size and constitution. Magma pockets would have to work their way up from the metal-rich depths to the outer crust. Then they would have to come into contact with materials which would dissolve or precipitate, as might be the case, the particular metals he sought.

The geological processes that depended so heavily on water or ammonia, in the liquid state, and concentrated the metallic compounds into ore deposits, could occur only near the surface. Of course, a magma pocket, commencing five hundred miles down, may not go upward. It may travel in any direction whatever, or not at all.

The density, the chemical composition, the melting point of the surrounding material, its ability to retain, in solution, the radioactives which may have been responsible for the pocket in the first place were all vital factors. Equally vital was the question of whether its crystalline makeup is such as to absorb or release energy as increasing temperature reorganizes it—the proximity of one or more of the vast iron-pockets, whose coreward settling contributes its share of energy. All of these things influence the path as well as the very existence of the pocket.

It would be relatively easy to predict, on a purely statistical basis, the number of ore-bodies to be formed in a given ten-million-year period. But the agent needed much more than that. When a freighter is dispatched to pick up metal at one specific point and deliver it to another, the schedule is apt to suffer, if the ship has to wait a million years for its load. Interrupted schedules are not merely nuisances. In a civilization spread throughout the core of the galaxy, none of whose member worlds are self-sufficient, they can be catastrophic.

So the agent measured carefully, and, as he did so, something a trifle queer began to appear. Impulses that did not quite fit into the orderly pattern he had deduced kept arriving—impulses of a nature he found, at first, hard to believe.

Then he remembered that the poachers had been here for quite a while before his own arrival, and an explanation lay before him. The impulses were of the sort that his own hull must have broadcast, while he was digging his present refuge. There could be only one thing that the poachers would logically have left behind them. They could have left evidence of their digging.

They had shown, he decided, a rather unusual amount of foresight for their kind, coupled with a ruthlessness that made the agent wonder whether they had even felt the radar beams that had greeted his own arrival. What the poachers had done was *not* a thing to do to an inhabited planet.

The out-of-place impulses were from mole robots, slowly burrowing their way into the world's heart. Each one, as the agent patiently computed its position, course, and speed, was headed for a point where the release of a relatively minute amount of energy would swing delicately balanced forces in a particular direction. The direction was obvious enough. The poachers expected to be back for another load, and were stimulating Earth's diastrophic forces to provide it.

This was a technique often used by legitimate metal-producers, but only on worlds that were uninhabited. Orogeny, even when stimulated in this fashion, may take half a million years to raise a section of landscape a few thousand feet. That still would not provide time to escape for beings who, without mechanical assistance, would take something like the same length of time to travel a few hundred.

From the agent's point of view, the presence of such depth-charges meant that Earth was going to become, in a fairly short time, a writhing, buckling, seething surface of broken rock, molten lava and folding, crumpling, tilting rafts of silicate material on a fearfully disturbed sea of stress-fluid.

Such heartless behavior might prove unavoidable—since he wouldn't be there at the time. But—what had produced those radar beams?

It revolted him that any planet with life should be treated in such a manner. Whether or not the life was currently intelligent was beside the point. Few generations were needed to transform a life species, from something as unresponsive as the planet that had spawned them, into a species capable of understanding the internal mechanism of a star in detail, for any distinctions of that nature to carry weight. If those beams had originated from living bodies, something would have to be done about the moles.

The agent simply had not the equipment to do a thing. He could fight his little ship. He could investigate and analyze. He could communicate all the way across the galaxy, if something like the ionized layers of a planet's atmosphere did not interfere.

But he had no mole robots on his vessel, no weapons that would penetrate rock, or even atmosphere, for any great distance. He could not himself stand the temperatures at depths to which some of the poacher's moles had already penetrated. Consequently, he could not follow them in his own ship, even if it were able to dig as rapidly as the robots. It was indeed a problem!

Sending for help was possible, but almost certainly useless. His patrol area was so far out near the galactic rim that any message would take several millennia to reach a point where it would do any good—and the ships which answered it would be at least three times as long in covering the distance as the radiation that summoned them.

By then most, if not all, of the robots would have reached their designated target points. They would have shut off the fields that held their shape against the pressure of the surrounding rock. Once that protection was gone, no material substance in the universe could keep the half-ton of fissionable isotopes forming their cargoes at sub-critical separation. All that energy would come out, and the little that wasn't heat to start with soon would be.

Of course, even such amounts of energy are small in comparison with the usual supplies of a planet's crust. But once released in carefully calculated spots and at even more carefully calculated times they would do exactly what the poachers wanted. The Conservation agent, checking the placement of the moles, could find no fault with the computations of the poachers' geophysicist. He was in his own way an operator of genius!

He could, of course, arrange for official freighters to be on hand when the action bore fruit, and would certainly do so, as a last resort. But he must first attack the question of whether or not life was being endangered. For the first time since the beginning of his analysis, the agent directed his attention to the surface layers of the world.

Then he almost stopped again, as a new theory struck him. This planet had free oxygen in its atmosphere. Would its life, if any, be near the surface? But his hesitation was only momentary. He recalled the radar beams that were his only reason for suspecting life. They could not possibly have passed through any significant amount of rock. While his senses swept the surrounding crust, in ever-widening circles, he pondered the question of just how a living creature could endure such an environment. *Think hard now—concentrate!*

There was one obvious possibility. It might be riding a machine designed to protect it, as he was himself—which would imply that life was not native to this world. If that were the case, locating the creature or creatures should be easy. However, in such circumstances it would have to be assumed that the population was very small, since furnishing machines for all of a large population was a manifest impossibility. It would be unwise too—even if such a thing *were* possible.

A more fantastic idea was that, while the life of this world might have a carbon composition like his own, its metallic parts were of more inert substances—perhaps of the platinum-group metals. The agent knew no reason why these should not serve as well as calcium, in a nervous system. He might have thought of aluminum, had he been familiar with its behavior in an oxygen-water environment.

Then, there was the notion that a ship of his own race might be down and crippled-the most fantastic of all. No such ship would be this far out in the galaxy, and it was hard to imagine a mishap which would leave the operator alive and safe from the environment, while crippling his communication facilities to the point where nothing but crude whistles came through.

Furthermore, there had been too many points of origin for the beams that had touched him. It might prove a difficult nut to crack.

In fact, it was simply impossible to decide whether one of these hypotheses, or something that had not yet occurred to him would prove closest to the truth. For the time being there was nothing to do but search. Naturally, it did not take long for the more or less rhythmic impulses originating only a few miles away to catch his attention.

They were seismic, of course, since he was doing all his listening through the rock—but it quickly became evident that they were originating at the very boundary between lithosphere and atmosphere. Almost as quickly, he realized that the sources were moving.

This latter fact complicated the analysis rather seriously. It took the agent some time to conclude that sets of more or less solid objects, apparently always in pairs, were striking the lithosphere from outside. Sometimes there were relatively long periods of regular, repeated thuds, as one or more of the pairs did its hammering and such periods were always accompanied by motion of the point at which the blows were occurring.

At other times, the hammering was irregular, both in frequency and energy, and usually, though not always, these sequences radiated from a relatively fixed broadcasting point. There seemed to be six basic units producing the impulses. Well, he was making progress, at any rate. Systematic thought could be a joy in itself!

Quite evidently, if this disturbance were caused by local life, that life must be civilized to the point where it could design and build machines. Furthermore, six machines, machines so close together, really did call for thought. It suggested something about the population density of the planet.

On the worlds the agent knew, scarcely one individual in a thousand manned a machine capable of moving him about. To equip the rest similarly would not only be the height of folly. It would be impossible, because enough material could never be obtained, still more because very few of them were temperamentally suited to physical activity. Even if this race had equipped, say, one in a hundred of its members, the finding of such a number congregated in one spot implied either a tremendous population density or—*could it be that they were looking for him?*

He had never stopped to think what a two-dimensional search would be like. But these machines, he was beginning to think, must be confined to surface-travel—perhaps sub-surface as well—and their operators were assuming that he was on or near the surface of the lithosphere.

The agent cast his memory back over the paths these

things had been following, and decided that they might indeed be explained on the assumption they were seeking something and had a very restricted range of sensory perception. He dwelt for an instant on the last assumption, finding it unpleasant.

The radar beams, then, must have been used to track him. He had felt no such impulses, since digging in, although a portion of his hull remained exposed. But his attention had been so completely taken up with his work that he might not have noticed. He began to listen more carefully for electromagnetic radiation, and heard it immediately. On the instant, any doubts that might have remained concerning the intelligence of this race were disposed of.

There was a single source, which seemed to accompany only one of the machines, though the agent found it a little harder to locate precisely than the seismic sources. Apparently radio waves were being reflected from surfaces not in his mental picture of this part of the planet, thus confusing slightly his attempts at orientation. He was disturbed by the seeming fact that only one of these operators talked—and wondered why there had been no answer.

That problem was quickly solved, however. More careful listening disclosed a response coming from a fixed point some distance away. The agent did not attempt to make a seismic check on the environs of this source of radiation, since there was already enough to occupy his attention.

Still, why should only one of these machines, or its driver, be engaged in long-range conversation? Surely the others, if they were fit to be trusted to drive such devices, must occasionally have ideas of their own. It did not occur to him that the impulses might not represent speech—their pattern complexity was too great for anything else, though their tone was rather monotonous—quite literally. The frequency was constant and only the amplitude was modulated.

One possibility, of course, was that there was only one operator present, who was reporting to or discussing matters with his more distant fellow while he controlled all six of the nearby machines. In that case, however, the impulses he was using to control the subsidiary vehicles should be detectable, and nothing of the sort had reached the agent's senses.

Could it be that the orders were transmitted by metallic connections instead of radiation? They would have to be flexible, of course, since the relative positions of the machines were constantly changing! Yes, that could be it!

CHAPTER FOUR

Candace Parsons prepared dinner that night in the larger tent, over the fire-less cooker. Because, for all of her native independence of spirit, she enjoyed being a woman and Hal's wife, and because she found herself not yet able, either intellectually or emotionally, to accept what had happened to them during the day, she concentrated on preparing the best meal possible under the circumstances.

While Hal and Truck continued to work the radio, under the trailer tarpaulin, she opened a couple of cans of chili, reinforced their contents with extra powder and placed on the stove a panful of the nourishing Mexican dish. She got a pot of coffee smoking, fried a dozen quarter-inch thick slices of bacon, and stirred the heated chili. Then she carried out to the men large, steaming platefuls of the rib-sticking food. They looked, she thought, as damp as she felt.

Returning with the coffee, she found the plates barely touched and told them, "You'd better eat hearty, characters. Heaven only knows when I'll cook another mess in this downpour."

Hal looked at her sheepishly, turned away from the transmitter and picked up his plate. "Sorry, baby," he said. "But, whatever this is all about, we seem to be it. We've had about everybody but the President on the air, asking us what in hell is going on."

"Let me take over for a while," she urged.

Truck, temporarily deserting his chore at the crank-battery to consume his victuals in what appeared to be three immense mouthfuls, said, "I'm afraid, memsahib, that this is going to be an all-night beat."

It turned out to be just that, since a baffled, excited, curious, and somewhat frightened world refused to leave them alone. Increasingly, it became apparent that no other observer, human or electronic, had spotted further passage of the mysterious flying object that Truck called "the Greatest Whatisit." Thus, until the rain let up and the ceiling lifted, the Parsons Expedition was definitely roped down, and committed.

And the rain, as Candace had foreseen, did not let up. That, in and of itself, was one of the most unusual elements in the situation. According to all reports, the storm that had engulfed them extended over no more than a few square miles, centering upon the valley, and its surrounding territory.

The circumstance caused Truck to suggest, "Well, a limited storm area ought to simplify things. All they'll have to do now is locate the center of the cloud region. The center will be it—granted our Whatisit is seeding the clouds around here with malicious intent."

"How could it seed clouds that didn't even exist until after it came down?" queried Candace.

"So it made its own clouds," Truck suggested breezily. "Take it or leave it."

Candace and Hal Parsons exchanged a puzzled look. It was Parsons who got to his feet. They were sitting, Turkish fashion, on the ground beneath the larger tent's shelter and Parsons arose quickly to say, "Never mind the battery for a moment, Truck. Where's that Geiger counter of yours?"

"You mean to say you're gonna hunt uranium *now?*" Truck asked good-humoredly, as he complied.

"Not exactly," said Hal Parsons, a trifle grimly. "Okay, Truck—thanks." Neither he nor Candace felt up to putting into words the way they felt about the fear that gripped them. Any object capable of emitting radiations that could create such a furious local storm might well be capable of emitting radiations deadly to all human life within its radius. Both had visions of the Japanese fishermen who, in 1955, were caught in a radioactive fallout hundreds of miles from the Eniwetok atomic testing grounds.

Candace carried the electric lantern as Hal made his way about fifty feet downhill, into the saddle of the pass where they were encamped. She heard the ominous click-click-click of the counter, as her husband turned it on, and caught the strange, tense look on his features—a look sharpened by rainwater and the lantern's bright beam. She had an odd, shafting thought that this was not her husband at all, but a stranger. Quickly she closed mental lock and key on the idea, lest it be a prelude to panic.

He said, "It's high, but that might be caused by any number of reasons."

Candace nodded, and he took a few more strides. Then he bent low over a large puddle, formed in a hollow of the ground, and held the counter directly over it. The speed of the clicking increased by a clearly audible margin. After a moment, he stood up, and turned the instrument off.

"We're okay," he said. "The rain is radioactive, all right. But, unless we hang around here for a month or two, it's not likely to cause any permanent damage."

"It can't damage *my* permanent," she replied. "I haven't had one in six months, and the coil came out in a week." The moment she had spoken, she felt like an idiot for making such a remark at such a time. On the other hand, she thought, this might be a moment when idiocy could really serve a purpose.

Hal said gently, "Shut up, baby," and then they walked back to the camp in silence, their minds full of oddly parallel thoughts, hopes, and fears. Increasingly, via radio and their own evidence, it was becoming clear that the Whatisit had elected to come to earth nearby, and probably knew exactly what it was doing.

"You know," said Hal, after lighting a damp cigarette, "if our friend had such a thought in mind, he couldn't have figured out a better way to stay clear of observation. Locating him on foot, in this rain, is going to be next to impossible. And the authorities outside the area won't find it easy to get in here. Our trail is washed out by this time. In fact, for all we know, the valley behind us will be flooded by morning. They can't observe from the air, because of the clouds—and the ceiling is so low I don't believe a helicopter could make a landing anywhere near here."

"Maybe he *does* want to," said Candace, re-lighting her cigarette thoughtfully.

"But that suggests…" Hal looked at her oddly.

"It suggests intelligence, all right," his wife said quickly. "And so did the swift, sure way he steered a path around this mountain yesterday. The big question now is—what *kind* of intelligence?"

"You're giving me the creeps," said Hal. He looked at her in the light of the electric lantern and smiled. But there was no mirth in his smile and when her hand crept toward his along the moist ground, he gripped it almost eagerly.

Truck MacLaurie stood over them. "If you two lovebirds are interested," he said, "I just got word they're sending a plane over in five minutes, to try to drop a flare through the clouds. They'll want to know if we can see it—and where."

The Parsons' scrambled to their feet and waited, by the radio, as the minutes ticked by. An eternity seemed to pass before they actually heard the distant drone of the plane. It grew rapidly louder and, all at once, appeared to be almost directly overhead. The receiver crackled, and Hal Parsons took over.

"You're coming in," he told them. "Parsons here. Over."

"Roger, Professor," came the buoyant voice of the airman overhead. "We're dropping a flare in five seconds. You should see her in twenty-six, when she blossoms. If you spot any little green men, let us know."

"Fire away," said Parsons. He frowned and added tersely: "And stop clowning."

"Roger dodger," was the reply, and Parsons wished, briefly, that the over-carefree birdman had to take the brunt on the ground with them. Then he recalled Candace's inane remark about her permanent, and it occurred to him that some people found such flipness an antidote to unendurable tension. He waited...

The flare burst, no more than half a mile away, its brilliance muted by the heavy mist and rainfall. Of the valley itself, it revealed almost nothing. Then, slowly, it burned out, leaving the darkness darker than before.

Parsons reported it, not too exactly under the circumstances, and the pilot said, "Well, that tells us exactly what we knew before. Stay with it, Professor."

Curiously, Parsons thought, he sounded discouraged.

Morning dawned, gray and soggy. But even so, the three on the mountain pass were lifted up in spirit by the renewal of light. The rain continued, without letup, and patches of mist clung to the slopes above and below them—and as far as their vision could penetrate.

They breakfasted on fresh coffee and the warmed-up remnants of the meal they had been unable to finish the night before.

"I never thought I'd have a miniature lake to wash dishes in," said Candace, dipping the plates in a puddle of fresh rainwater, and wiping them dry with a towel. "I've always had to scrub plates with sand on trips like this."

"Yeah," said Truck MacLaurie, "and radioactive rainwater,

at that."

"Shut up, Truck," Hal Parsons said sharply, wishing he had held his tongue. It occurred to him, for the first time in his life, that people who can face grim reality and joke about it are, perhaps, far better realists than those who regard it so seriously that even talk of it disturbs them. What was troubling him was not the fact that the rain was mildly radioactive. It was the possibility that the great Whatisit might be emanating radiations of an alien nature, and more deadly to humans than anything the Geiger counter could pick up. Ignoring Candace's silent reproof, he walked slowly to the jeep.

Even though the slope into the valley was not steep, getting down the western side of the pass proved a far more difficult task than hauling the jeep up the east side had been. The reason, of course, was the unremitting rain, which was turning the poorly fastened dirt-and-sand hillside surface into treacherous, slippery rivers of silt and mud.

On this part of the trip Truck rose to heroic effort. Almost at the valley floor the little vehicle unexpectedly side-slipped into a freshly made brook, causing its rear wheels to stick and the trailer to fall over on its side. In a matter of seconds, the big football player had leapt from the rear seat of the jeep into the shin-deep muck, and was heaving at the trailer, with his neck cords swelling.

Before Hal or Candace could reach him he had unlocked the coupler and was hauling an upright trailer out of the water by main strength.

"The tarp held tight," he said cheerfully, not even panting. With his hair plastered over his forehead and his clothes clinging to him in the wet, he looked as if he had just stepped out of a shower with his clothes on. He added smilingly: "Get behind that wheel, Doc, while I push."

It took their combined efforts, but they finally got the jeep clear of the water and back on reasonably firm soil. Candace returned to the shelter of the jeep-top, while Hal and Truck re-coupled the trailer.

Feeling thoroughly ashamed of himself for his previous sharpness, Hal said, "Truck, I'm sorry if I've been riding roughshod over you, but this whole business has me on edge. I mean, with Candace, and—" He let it hang.

Truck laid a massive, damp hand on Hal's already soaked shoulder and said with a grin, "Doc, don't worry about me. I've been chewed out by so many coaches giving me hell in the locker room that I don't mind a little ribbing from a guy I respect."

For some reason, the atmosphere lightened, though the rain continued to fall—and, curiously, the going grew easier from then on. Twenty minutes later, they had reached the floor of the valley, which extended almost level into the mist that blocked the mountains on the further side.

"Well," said Truck from the rear seat, as Hal slowly brought the jeep to a halt, "now that we're here, what do we do?"

The Parsons exchanged a look. Until then, reaching the valley had loomed as so large a problem in front of them that they had not considered the next move.

Candace laughed and said, "I'd pause at this point to powder my face if it would do any good in the dampness—if I had any powder handy."

To his considerable surprise, Hal found himself paraphrasing a long-forgotten and very ribald old Negro ditty that by rights should have remained buried in the rather scant excesses of his youth. He said, "It's right here for us, and if we don't find it, why it ain't no fault of its."

"Hey, Doc!" said Truck. "Where'd you pick that one up?"

"Probably," said Candace dryly, "in the very place where he picked me up."

It was the younger man who spoke seriously then. "No fooling, folks," Truck said. "Now that we're here, just how do we go about *finding* our inhuman friend? Don't forget—you're the brains in this pitch. I'm just the muscle."

"I'm afraid we're going to have to use that Geiger counter of yours again," Hal Parsons said. "And no cracks, please. If we can find any variation of intensity in the rainfall radiation, there may be a chance..."

"Gotcha, Doc." Again, the young Goliath was out of the jeep, and working at the trailer tarpaulin.

"Do you think it will work, honey?" Candace asked.

Hal Parsons shrugged. "It might," he said. "It just might."

But it didn't. As remorselessly as the rain continued to fall, the mild radioactivity continued to register without variation. After testing puddles for two hours, the two men returned to the jeep, where Candace had coffee ready for them once more. She asked no questions as to the success of their experiment. One look at their faces as they emerged from the mist told her all she needed to know.

"Carnotite," said her husband, lifting his face from an empty tin cup and wiping his mouth on his sleeve. "Not enough to report on—just enough to bitch us up for an hour, with a false lead. You might not believe it, but this is one hell of a big valley."

"It keeps getting bigger," said Truck mournfully through a coffee mustache. He looked at Hal and asked, "Well, Doc—what next?"

Hal was trying to come up with some sort of a constructive reply, when Candace motioned for him to be silent and lifted her face upward. The others followed her gaze and saw nothing but clouds, rain and fog. Then they heard it—the drone of a plane directly overhead. Without a word, both men handed Candace their empty cups and moved toward the trailer.

It was a mere matter of minutes, before they had the radio back in action, and were trying to communicate with the crew overhead. While Truck cranked away at the battery, to raise power, Parsons hung onto the transmitter, urgently repeating, "Parsons calling plane. Parsons calling plane. We hear you. We hear you. Come on in. Come on in. Over..."

All he could get, on the earphones, was a rumble of static, through which—now and again—he heard the faint, unintelligible mutter of the operator upstairs, trying to break through. Candace looked at him anxiously, her hair oddly slicked into bangs by the rain. He shook his head hopelessly.

"Keep trying," she said softly. "Keep trying, Hal honey."

Frustration was high within him, but he nodded and tried again. "Parsons calling plane. Parsons calling plane," he began.

This time, there was no doubt about the answer. It came, clear as a voice in some un-built next room, saying, "Parsons calling plane. Parsons calling plane."

"Who's that?" he barked, recalling the impertinence of the aircraft radio message of the night before.

"Who's that?" he barked. *"Hello?"*

"Who's that? *Hello?"* the mocking voice replied.

Parsons mopped rainwater out of his eyes and snapped, "What in hell is going on? This isn't funny, Mack!"

And the voice replied, "What in hell is going on? This isn't funny, Mack!"

"Cut it out, you joker!" he said furiously. "If you've got a message for us, unload it and take off."

To which his tormentor retorted, "Who's that? *Hello?"*

"Hal honey!" interposed Candace, who had crowded close and turned back one of the earphones to catch the mocking message. "Hal honey, he's replying in *your* voice."

"So what?" her husband countered. "Whoever he is, I'm

going to see he gets hell—once we're out of here."

"Just a second." She nudged him clear of the transmitter, bent over the mouthpiece, and said clearly, "Toodle-oo, old thing."

The answer came back clear as spoken—and in perfect reproduction of Candace's voice. "Toodle-oo, old thing."

They stared at each other until Truck came over. He pushed back his hair and said, "What is this—a private game, or can anybody play?"

"It's beginning to look," said Hal quietly, his controlled voice belying the wild excitement in his eyes, "as if your great Whatisit is as anxious to get in touch with us as we are with him." Then, turning to Candace, he asked, "What do you think, baby?"

"I think," she said, "if I were an alien and wanted to be a radio announcer and could only receive H. V. Kaltenborn, I'd give it back to him just the way he was giving it to me."

CHAPTER FIVE

IT BECAME INCREASINGLY evident to the Conservationist that he could lie there, until he was trapped in an earthquake, making up five hundred theories per second, without getting one whit closer to knowledge of what was happening around him. He was going to have to examine the machines more closely. The only question was one of tactics. Should he go to them, or have them come to him?

He decided first to try the second gambit, since it offered more promise of drawing out information as to their nature and abilities. He would thus be able to determine precisely what stimuli affected their senses of equipment, and the extent of their capability in analyzing what they did detect.

Naturally, not a wave of their radiation had, thus far, conveyed any meaning to the Conservationist. More accurately, the few patterns that even remotely matched patterns of his own language did not deceive him for an instant by such chance similarities. Nor did he suppose the natives would have any better luck with his language.

His first attempt at attracting their attention consisted merely of broadcasting sustained notes on a variety of frequencies, other than the one they were using. As he had rather expected, these produced no noticeable reaction. Travel and conversation went on unaffected. When he repeated the attempts, using the same wavelength as the natives, however, the results were just as unsatisfactory. It was extremely frustrating.

Travel stopped, and after he had repeated the signal a few

times, all six of the vehicles seemed to come together at one spot. In the pauses between his own transmissions, the native speech sounded almost continuously. Yet he felt doubt that he had even been heard.

He had rather expected that there might be an attempt to respond to him in kind, but this did not occur, even though he tried sending out his wave in various long and short pulses, which should have been easy to copy. At least, he used lengths corresponding to those of the radar pulses that he had felt at his arrival, and which had, presumably, been emitted by members of this race.

They failed to respond to the patterns, however, even when in desperation he increased the lengths of the bursts of radiation to three or four thousand microseconds. The very speech patterns of the natives changed carrier amplitude in shorter periods than that—they must, he felt, be able to distinguish such intervals!

The agent began to speculate upon the general intelligence-level of this alien new race. He had to remind himself forcibly that, since they could move around so rapidly, they must be able to design and build complex machines. It was startling, to say the least.

Then it occurred to him that all the vehicles he was watching might be remote controlled, that the electromagnetic waves he was receiving were the control impulses. Yes, yes, that must be it! He spent some time, trying to correlate the radio signals with the motions of the machines. The attempt, of course, failed completely, since men are at least as likely to talk while standing still, as while walking around.

This proving a poor check on his hypothesis—it did not disprove it, since the machines might be able to do many things besides move around—he tried duplicating some of their complete signal groups, watching carefully to see whether any motion of the vehicles resulted. He realized that the controlling entity might not like what he was doing, but he was sure that satisfactory explanations could be made, once contact was established.

The result of the experiment was a complete stoppage of motion, as nearly as he could tell. It was not quite what he had expected. But there was some gratification in getting any result at all. For several whole seconds there was silence, both seismic and electromagnetic.

Then the native speech—it had to be speech—began again, in groups which still seemed long to the agent, but which were certainly much shorter than most of those used before. He duplicated each group as it came.

"Who's that? *Hello?*"

"Who's that? *Hello?*"

"What in hell is going on? This isn't funny, Mack!"

"What's going on? This isn't funny, Mack."

"Cut it out, you joker! If you've got a message for us, unload it and take off!"

"Who's that? Hello?" The agent decided the last signal group was too long to be worth imitation, so he went back to one of the earlier groups. This action resulted in brief silence, followed by a pattern, brief, but with a fresh modulation, which he mimicked accurately. For several whole minutes, the conversation, if it could be called that, went on. He felt real pride now, a self-congratulatory kind of exaltation in being able to carry off his cleverly assumed masquerade with perfect confidence, vigor and, certainly, no small measure of success.

The Conservation agent had decided long since what the native machines would almost certainly do, and was pleased to detect them getting into motion once more. But when they had gone far enough for him to determine their direction of travel, he discovered, with some disappointment, that they were not moving toward him.

He would have had little trouble solving their motives, had they been moving straight *away* from him. But the angle they took carried them more or less in his direction, albeit considerably to one side. He found this a complete mystery, at first. Finally he noticed that the group was traveling along a depressed portion of the lithosphere's surface, and seized upon, as a working hypothesis, the idea that their machines found it difficult, or impossible, to climb slopes of more than a few degrees.

In that case, of course, they might not be able to reach him, directly or otherwise, since he had buried himself some distance up the side of a valley. He considered again leaving his position and coming to meet them, but reached the same decision as before—that he could learn more by seeing what they did on their own.

They spoke rarely as they traveled—but the agent found that he could always make them broadcast, by ceasing to radiate his own signal. Had they not been pursuing such an odd course, he would have supposed, from that fact, that they were using his radiation to lead them to him. His radiation! However, they kept on their course until they were somewhat past its nearest point to his position before they paused. Then there was a brief interchange of signals with some distant native, apparently in an atmosphere machine, and travel was resumed, at right angles to the original direction.

Now, however, the vehicles were heading away from the buried ship. They had, in fact, turned left. The Conservationist gave up theorizing for the moment and contented himself with observing. He repressed his mounting excitement and became as still as a figure of stone.

They did not travel very far in the new direction. In less than half an hour they stopped again, held another brief conversation, and then began to retrace their steps to, and finally across, their original route. Apparently, they were still interested in the agent's broadcasts. At any rate, they continued repeating the early "Hello" and "Who's that" signals to which he had originally responded, whenever he stopped radiating. They were not following the radiation, but certainly—almost certainly—they had some interest in it.

Then, quite abruptly, they stopped traveling and appeared to lose interest in the whole matter. The group broke up, and its members wandered erratically about for some time. Then they drew together once more and gradually quieted down completely, or at least to the point where the agent could not be sure that the occasional impulses coming from that area were due to their motion.

He had just developed another theory, and this new trick bothered him seriously. He would have preferred to ignore it, but he could not. It had occurred to him that these creatures might be able to detect electromagnetic radiation of the sort he had been broadcasting, but not be able to identify the direction from which it came. He had heard of cases of physical injury among his own people that had produced such a result.

The idea that such a disability might be universal in this race called for a severe stretch of the agent's imagination, but he toyed with it all the same. As a result, he had just come to realize that the peculiar motions of the things he had been observing could indeed be accounted for by the assumption that they were searching for him under some such handicap—when they stopped moving. This was hard to reconcile with any sort of search procedure. What possible reason could stop them? He wished sometimes there could be fewer complexities in his existence. What possible reason?

Lack of fuel? Inconceivable, assuming even minimum intelligence on the part of the operator or operators.

Surface impossible for the machines to travel over? Unlikely, since several of them had come some distance toward him during their erratic wandering after the halt of the main body. And there had been others in the atmosphere.

Sun-powered mechanisms, halted by the fact that night had fallen? It was possible, though it seemed a trifle odd for such a device to be used on a rotating planet, where it must be sunless half the time. Also, it seemed doubtful that the machines were large enough to intercept the requisite amount of solar radiation. The agent had a fair idea of their size and mass, from the minimum observed separation, plus the energy with which they struck the ground.

Not interested in him at all, and stopped simply because they had reached their intended destination? This seemed all too painfully probable, if the course of their travels were considered by itself—yet nearly impossible, if their reaction to his broadcasting were taken into account.

It was at this point that the agent began to consider seriously the possibility that he might never be able to get the information of their danger across to the inhabitants of this far-off planet. Their behavior, up to the present, definitely seemed to lack any element he could recognize as common sense. He was open-minded enough to realize that this might work both ways, yet such a possibility did not augur well for the chances of successful communication between the two intelligences involved. There were cynics even among his own people who claimed that folly arid ignorance always went arm in arm, and were biological constants throughout space.

Once more, he was facing the question of whether he should go to meet these gadgets or wait where he was—and, in the latter case, how long he should wait. Certainly, if he were to check the possibility that they were sun-powered, he should not stir until after night was over.

But none of the other hypotheses could very well be tested without actually examining, at close hand, the natives and their machines. He decided, then, to wait until sunrise, and for a reasonable period thereafter. Then, if these things did not resume their journey in his general direction, he would seek them out.

As it turned out, he did not have to move. The appearance of the sun saw the vehicles already in motion, which was informative in a negative way. After a brief period of random traveling, they congregated once more, seemed to confer silently for a time, and then resumed travel along their former route. Also, they broadcast once more the signal the agent had come to interpret as a request for him to start transmitting.

The events of the preceding afternoon were repeated in some detail. The group continued past the agent's station on their straight-line course for a short distance, then stopped, and once more made a right-angle turn. This time, it was to the right, toward the hidden alien—and the agent realized that this theory about their sensory limitations must be at least partly correct.

They had to go through elaborate maneuvers to locate the source of a radio broadcast—maneuvers that suggested that even their ability to judge the intensity of the radiation was rather crude. It took them about a tenth of the planet's rotation period, this time, to narrow the field down as far as their radio senses appeared to permit.

Before mid-morning they had made two more right-angle turns, and then spread out to cover, individually, the remaining area of uncertainty. The agent settled comfortably in his hole and awaited discovery. This should tell him much.

Just how close would these things have to come to detect him directly? Would he be able to pick up their nerve-currents first? What would they do when they found him?

How long would it take them to realize that he was not a native of their world? And, most important, would they have some constructive ideas about means of communication? Who did he think he was fooling? At the moment the agent would have admitted to anyone that he himself had none. And if he was up against a blank wall in that respect, how could he reasonably expect them to come up with something really new and brilliant?

He kept his own senses keyed up, striving to detect the first clue, other than radio and seismic waves, of the nearness of the Earthly machines. Presumably, they were more or less electrical in their nature, and he knew that electric and magnetic fields must, sooner or later, draw close enough to give him a picture of their structure. A little closer than that, and the electric fields of the operators' nervous systems should permit him to deduce their shapes and structures— assuming, of course, that at least one operator was with the present group of machines, which could hardly yet be considered certain.

Although it was the machine with the radio that actually stumbled on the buried vessel, the radio was not in use at the time. As a result, the agent decided, rather quickly, that no operator was in fact present. The radio was, of course, put to use the moment the ship was sighted—but its structure and nature was obvious to the alien, and it was quite evidently not an intelligent being.

It was, however, the only object in the vicinity with functioning, electrical circuits. Moreover, there was no direct sign of life in any of the machines that gathered quickly around the ship. Finding it a little hard to believe even his own theories, the agent once more examined the radio—only to reach the same conclusion.

Its organization was not sufficiently complex to compare with a single living crystal, much less an entire nervous system. The conclusion seemed inescapable. Not only was the machine carrying it being controlled from a distance, but even the vehicle itself operated *without detectable electrical forces*.

The machine, of course, could not be invisible. His failure to see it meant merely that he was employing the wrong means—*anything* material can be seen, in some way or other. There remained the question of just what were the proper means in this particular case.

Free metals affected electric or magnetic fields, or both, in ways that permitted their recognition. Only a few fragments of such material were present—fragments quite evidently shaped by intelligence, but not themselves part of either an intelligent body, or even a complex mechanism.

Non-conducting crystals reflected and refracted many kinds of radiation. Perhaps these things, then, could be *seen*. The only trouble with this idea was that eyes were not a normal part of the agent's physical makeup. While his ship possessed several which were used in navigation—stars were most easily detected and recognized by light waves—they all happened to be underground at the moment. He had never anticipated a use for them on the surface of the planet, not being himself a chemist.

The machines were now all moving about on the ground in his immediate vicinity. One of them even moved onto the exposed section of his hull for a few moments and it gave him his first chance to approximate their mass really accurately. Unfortunately he could not determine precisely how much of the energy radiating from their footsteps was due to weight.

The machine on his hull carried a tiny ionization tube, whose behavior at the moment was being affected by the mild radioactivity of the ship—activity only natural after a million years in interstellar space. The purpose of the tube was no more obvious than that of the electromagnetic radiator. Neither could move or think. The only possibility seemed to lie in a connection with the remote control of these machines. Perhaps, they were sensing devices of some sort.

There seemed no logical reason for not raising the ship far enough to get a look at these alien machines. He had discovered all he could expect to learn, from where he was. They *did* receive him. They *were* interested, and they, therefore, had at least glimmerings of intelligence. They could not—or, at least, their machines could not—determine the direction from which radio waves were coming.

It was still not clear to him whether these machines were under the control of one individual, or that of several. There seemed no way of investigating this important question for some time to come. What the agent wanted to know, as soon as possible, was just what sort of mechanism could operate *without perceptible electrical fields*—and that seemed to demand that he see them. Yes, he must see them.

His hull had long since cooled, and could be controlled without difficulty. He started it vibrating again, and, simultaneously, applied enough drive to counteract the weight of ship and its contents. For a fleeting instant, he wondered whether the distant operators could detect the flickering of the myriads of relays that responded to his thoughts, or even the electrical fields of the thoughts themselves.

If the latter were true, they could certainly not interpret them properly. In that case, the machines would have found him much earlier, and the agent would, by now, have been holding a conference with them about the best means of intercepting the mole robots. That possibility, he decided, could be ignored.

The patrol flier lifted easily, until over half its bulk was above the ground. Its pilot held it there, briefly, while the rhythm of the hull packed and firmed the powdered soil that had drifted beneath it. Then he cut his power once more, and began to look about him with his newly uncovered eyes.

CHAPTER SIX

THE LITTLE PARTY'S jubilation had proved short-lived. They had, it was true, attained communication with the Whatisit—but apparently all that it could or would do in this field was to mimic their voices and speech in startlingly unexpected fashion. After a quarter of an hour of ever-increasing exasperation, Truck MacLaurie won Parsons' temporary disfavor by suggesting, "Hey...I wonder if it can sing."

Candace didn't help the geologist's feelings by laughing outright at the infantile remark.

Hal said, "It's not funny, dammit! How are we going to get any more sense out of it? You'd think from the way you act this was a Sunday school picnic—not something deathly serious, even terrifying."

"I guess we'll have to find it first," said Truck, rubbing his face briefly dry with a large blue bandana. He looked more troubled and uneasy than he had permitted himself to look a moment before.

Candace gazed sadly at the ruin of her cigarette. "I wonder," she said, "just how we're going to accomplish that."

"Follow the beam," Truck suggested. He spoke lightly, but all the levity was gone from his stare.

"Get in," said Parsons, nodding toward the jeep. "We're going to find out if our friend really is beaming his messages."

They drove a quarter of a mile and tested. The baffling mimicry aped them just as clearly, just as strongly, as before.

"Maybe," said Candace optimistically, "we're headed straight toward him."

"Not likely, dear," said Parsons. But he got the jeep going

over the rough terrain at right angles to their previous direction before making another test. Once again, the mockery continued without any noticeable fluctuation in volume or alteration in its monotony of tone.

"Damn!" he exclaimed fervently. "He's sending without direction."

"What makes you so sure it's a him?" asked Candace.

"All right," said Hal, a trifle testily. *"She's* sending without direction."

"I didn't mean it that way, Hal honey," Candace told him. "I was just wondering if we hadn't jumped the gun in thinking of our friend as an intelligent entity."

"He, she or it was smart enough to move around that mountain yesterday," put in Truck, from the rear seat. "That took brains."

"Or machinery," said Candace. "Supposing its nothing more than a machine."

"That," said Hal, resting his forearms on the wheel in front of him, "raises some mighty interesting possibilities. Let's say, for the moment, that it is a machine. Obviously, a missile—if that's what it is—could have reactors that would enable it to avoid a crash—as with the mountain. But if it is a machine, somebody, or some *things,* had to make it. No intelligent creature would manufacture anything so complex without a purpose, and send it at random through space."

"Maybe it's not from space. Maybe the Commies sent it over to broadcast germs or something," said Truck.

"You think of the loveliest ideas," said Candace. Then, frowning and poking at the sopping ruin of her hair, "If that were true, it wouldn't be answering us—even with mockery. It would be lying nice and doggo. My money—listen to the girl!—says it's from space. If it were a missile that goofed, you can be sure the big brains in the Pentagon wouldn't be kicking up such a fuss."

"Well, we aren't going to solve the problem by sitting here talking about it," Hal said practically. "We've got to hunt until we find it."

"How are you going to do that?" Candace asked.

He told them. They were going to do it on foot, tracking the valley floor and leaving bits of cloth and direction markers whenever they reached the hills, so they would not be forced to retrace their steps. "That way," he concluded, "we can find out where it isn't, if nothing else."

"We can get good and wet, too," said Truck.

Parsons quelled him with a look, and they got busy. They hardly spoke at all, for their thoughts were now completely immediate, grim and serious.

It was a tedious, unrewarding day of plodding through rain-soaked sand and soil. When, as the sunless daylight waned, they finally returned to the shelter of the jeep, all three of them were exhausted.

"Another two or three days of this," Truck complained, "and my legs will be too muscle bound for football." It wasn't what he'd intended to say. It was merely a quick cover-up to conceal his real emotions.

"I think I left my feet on the other side of the valley, last time across," said Candace, falling in with his mood. "Hal honey, where do you suppose it is?"

"It's here somewhere," said Parsons, wishing his own feet would cool off and stop aching. "We just haven't looked in the right places."

"We'd better get back up a hill and do some broadcasting," said Candace. "I'll cook us some sort of a meal."

"I'm too tired to eat now," Parsons told her. "But you're right." He got the jeep into gear, adding, "Maybe they've found it somewhere else."

"Happy thought!" said Candace. "But it's too much to

hope for."

And theirs was the only report on the alien. Parsons talked to a General Somebody, who had jetted from Washington, D. C., to Butte that afternoon, to be closer to the critical scene. Apparently, the entire world was in a ferment over the possibility of contact with a messenger from an alien race.

"How are ground conditions?" the general asked.

"Lousy!" Parsons told him bluntly. He gave him a succinct account of the frustrating day the expedition had endured.

"You mean, you actually *talked* with it?" the General asked.

"You could call it that," said Hal, and went into a full explanation.

"Do you think we could get a helicopter in under those blankety-blank clouds?" the General wanted to know. "It would enable us to get a fix on its whereabouts."

Parsons looked dismally at the mist that enshrouded hilltop and valley alike. "Not a chance, I'm afraid," he said. "This stuff is thick and close. We're snafued, *but good!*"

Candace, who was standing by with a plate of hot food, heard this portion of the conversation and said, "Hal honey, maybe if they could get a plane overhead and they knew where we were, we could rig some sort of a fix on our friend. Ask him?"

"The trouble with that," said Parsons, "is our pal's sending doesn't reach up here. And how are we going to tell where either of us is if we can't see through the clouds?"

"What's that?" the General asked. "What's going on?"

"Mrs. Parsons," said Hal. "She wonders if you couldn't send a plane over tomorrow to help us get a radio fix on our friend."

There was silence. Then, "Tell your wife she gets a large box of filter-tip cigars when this is over. That's the first really constructive idea that's come out of this foul-up yet. But it will take a bit of doing. Lucky that stuff over you is not much more than two thousand feet. You'll hear from me in an hour. Signing off and good luck."

"What did he say?" Candace asked eagerly, as Parsons flipped the switch and motioned for Truck to stop cranking the battery.

"He says he's going to give you a box of choice Havana cigars when we get out of this hole, baby," Parsons told her, accepting his food. "Mmm! These beans are good! What did you do to them?"

"Oh—I just let you work up an appetite, that's all," said Candace. Then her eyes widened. "You mean he's actually going to do it?"

"He's going to try," said Hal through a full mouth. He tilted his tin plate to let the rainwater trickle off onto the ground. "If we ever do make sense with this creature, I'm going to ask him to turn off the waterworks."

"Amen to that!" said Candace.

"I was figuring on working up a sunburn that would last all winter," said Truck mournfully.

The general radioed back, on the nose. An air-fix would be attempted the following morning at ten o'clock. It was complicated, but he thought it could be done. "We've got to find that thing—or rather, you have to find it. Are you aware that we have an expedition with Weasels on its way to reinforce you?"

"Weasels!" Parsons was startled. "But we got in here okay in a jeep."

"You couldn't do it now," the general told him. "Those two days of wet weather have washed out all the trails. But don't worry. We'll be getting through to you soon. Just find our friend and see that he doesn't take off before we open communications."

"What's the verdict to date?" Parsons asked. "Is it extra-terrestrial?"

"Looks that way. The Russians swear on a stack of Karl Marx they had nothing to do with it. They're talking it up as some new sort of war-mongering frightfulness we've developed. Well, I'll be overhead tomorrow morning."

Once again, there was little sleep in the expedition. But their restlessness was not the result of frustration, unrewarding as their day of effort to locate the stranger had been. There was a sense of impending excitement, of discovery lying just ahead of them, a growing awareness of the importance of the position fate had put them in.

"If they're right," Candace mused aloud, "you and I, honey, are the first two humans ever to communicate with a being from another world."

"What price communication?" said Hal. "We might as well have been yelling our heads off in Echo Canyon."

"How about me?" put in Truck. "Don't I get to talk to it, too?"

"Of course, Truck!" Candace said warmly, reacting with quick, feminine sympathy to the young gladiator's sense of having been left on the outside. "You can talk your varsity team mask off tomorrow."

"Gee—thanks, memsahib," said Truck, feeling his dark inner mood lighten a little.

He retired into silence, apparently considering the effect of his impending importance on certain members of Candace's sex. She and Hal exchanged meaningful glances. They were both growing increasingly fond of Truck. He might not be cut out for a Ph.D., but his strength and stamina, his amiability and his quick native intelligence made him a valuable member of the closely-knit team they had become.

With the coming of the dawn, they rose and broke camp again. They made another descent to the valley floor, handling jeep and trailer with extra care lest an accident damage their radio gear. Certainly, weather-wise, the situation had not improved overnight. Mist and rain were equally heavy, and the once hard-packed ground was slowly turning into a quagmire. It took them more than an hour to get located on a bit of high ground, where they would not become hopelessly bogged down.

"Let's see if our friend is still sending," said Candace.

They set up shop, and Truck took over the mike. He said, "Hello, out there," and promptly received a "Hello, out there," in response.

Parsons scowled at the set. "If our pal doesn't shut up when the General starts sending," he said, "it's going to be awfully confused."

"We'll manage," Candace said confidently.

The general, as usual, was on time. He said, "I'm somewhere overhead in a helicopter, with another copter standing by. We want a fix on you, first. Then we'll try for a fix on the alien and at least give you direction."

"Hello out there," said the voice from the stars.

"Who in hell is that?" the general asked, startled.

"That," said Parsons, "is our unexplained visitor. You'll have to sift if he keeps cutting in."

"Okay, Parsons—let's get busy," said the general. "Start reeling off a page of statistics—or anything that comes into your head."

Parsons complied with the multiplication table. After imitating him at first, the Whatisit apparently gave up and stopped sending. Ten minutes later, the general's voice came over the receiver.

"We've got you," he said. "Now, see if you can get the owner of that voice."

Parsons raised the unknown visitor, using short, varied sentences. He was, he felt with growing excitement, beginning to learn a little about the alien. Two or three times, when the human speeches were long and intricate, or merely repetitious, it had simply ceased sending. Evidently, some sort of selective mind was at work, determining which phrases merited repetition, and which did not—even though, apparently, none of them made sense to the alien.

"Okay, Parsons, here it is," said the general. "Got a compass handy?" He gave the directions concisely, and concluded by saying, "Sorry we can't give you more. We spot you maybe half a mile apart, but our own location is too unstable to give you a clean estimate of distance. If you follow the direction I just gave you, and keep your eyes open, you ought to find him."

"We'll do our best, General," said Hal. Then, sighting along the direction-line he had just been given, he exclaimed in dismay, "Damn! This runs right along the hills on the north side of this bowl."

"You'll manage," said the general, with a confidence Hal, at that moment, was far from feeling. "Good luck. But be careful. He may be dangerous."

"Now he tells us," said Candace, who had appropriated one of the earphones.

They had to leave the jeep where it was, and scramble, slipping, stumbling, peering vainly through the mist for some sign of the alien. Their progress was abruptly halted when they had covered about a quarter of a mile, and the hillside across which they were moving became split by a sharp declivity.

"It couldn't be worse!" muttered Parsons. "We'll have to work our way around it."

Working their way around took them approximately half an hour. They were about halfway up the gentler slope of the far side when Truck, who had lumbered on ahead, let out a yell that echoed from crag to crag like a many-throated summons to battle.

"Here it is! I've found it! Come on, you two! *I've found it!*"

It was big. Although, in some unexplained manner, it had buried itself in the hillside, so that only a small sector of its top-surface showed above ground, the curve of its dull-gray, irregular and knotty metallic surface revealed a diameter of more than twenty feet. There it sat, immobile, apparently harmless—like a large piece of leaden-hued pewter discarded from a New England farmhouse attic.

"We found it! We *fou-ound it!*" Truck chanted, and then suddenly turned deathly pale, as the terrifying significance of the find's brooding stillness and nearness and alienness was borne in upon him.

"Get off at once!" Parsons almost shrieked the words. "You don't know what sort of radiations may be coming from it."

Truck swayed as if in mortal terror and scrambled down. "My God!" he breathed. "I left the Geiger counter back in the trailer."

"Get it," Parsons shot back to him. *"And get the jeep as close as you can."* Apparently whatever is inside that thing can only communicate through the radio."

"I know—sure," said Truck. "I—I'll be right back with the Geiger counter."

He had just turned to carry out the order, when Candace uttered a small shrill scream and cried, "Look! Hal, stay back! It's boiling the earth around it!"

Something very strange was happening. Invisible currents were making the once-sandy soil in which the object had settled seethe like boiling water in a kettle. As Parsons pulled his wife quickly away from the area of disturbance, he thought that her use of the word "boiling" had been singularly apt. From a safe distance up the hillside, the three of them watched the ground around the visitor act as solid matter was not supposed to act.

It was Truck who first sensed the visitor's intentions. Stabbing a large grimy forefinger at it he announced, "For pete's sake, he's coming up!"

They looked on in awe as the dull-gray globe that was not from Earth slowly emerged from its bed of soil, looming larger and larger as it rose, and revealing in what appeared to be its nose a pair of opaque, circular objects that looked like eyes.

CHAPTER SEVEN

THE STAR-TRAVELER already knew, of course, that he was in a valley, partway up one of the sides. The hills bounding it were not particularly high, especially by the standards of this planet. In fact, the Conservationist had a pretty accurate idea of the dimensions of the Himalayas, distant as they were—though he had been more interested in determining the rate at which they were rising. He gave the local elevations only a passing thought, then sought to examine what lay closer to his vision—outlets—outlets which the Parsons group had quite correctly labeled "eyes."

He failed. The details five miles away were clear and clouds of what must be water or ammonia droplets hanging at still greater distances in the atmosphere were still clearer. But, as he brought his attention to objects nearer and nearer to his ship, they grew, shapeless, and increasingly harder to examine.

Cursing himself for forgetting, he recognized the reason. His eyes were perfectly good instruments—for the purpose toward which they had been designed. They were carefully shaped lenses of calcium fluoride, designed with almost a full hemisphere of field and their curved focal surface was followed faithfully by the photosensitive material of his own flesh. The tiny metallic crystals in his stony tissues would, of course, be affected electrically by light, and, like many of his race, he had learned to interpret the light-images formed by lenses.

There was just one catch. There was no provision for changing either the shape or the position of the lenses. But actually, why should there be? They were designed to enable him to determine the directions of the stars, whose distances were for all practical purposes always infinite. He had never needed focusing arrangements until now.

The eyes were a foot across and almost as great in focal length. Objects a hundred yards away were blurs. At six feet they were scarcely interruptions to the background. He could just tell, by sight, that there were moving objects in his vicinity, and get a vague idea of their size. Beyond that, details were indistinguishable.

The nearest repair-shop where his machinery could be modified was about six thousand light-years toward the galactic center. He could, of course, pull his flesh back from one or more of the lenses until the eye involved focused at a distance of a few feet—if the situation would wait for the necessary years or centuries. However, even if the situation did wait, the natives and their machines probably wouldn't.

He could wait until they departed, and examine them when they were far enough away. Better than this, he could fly to a distance at which they were reasonably distinct in his sight. The question raised in that connection was, of course, how the natives would react to such a move on his part. However, if he did not move, he would probably learn nothing. Therefore, he resumed his rise from the soil, cleared its surface, and hurled his vessel half a mile upward.

To observe, and, in effect, to photograph the details of what lay below took only a few microseconds. Then he moved a few hundred yards to one side and repeated the procedure. Three seconds after takeoff, he was settling back into his original location with a fairly clear picture of the strange equipment surrounding it firmly painted in his mind.

He understood now why the seismic impulses had come in pairs. Each of the machines was supported by two struts, which were so hinged as to permit several degrees of freedom of motion. During his brief period of observation, they had traveled enough—away from the point where his ship had been resting—to permit him to analyze their startling method of travel. This seemed to consist in balancing on one strut, falling in the desired direction, and catching one's mass with the other before collapsing completely. The process was repeated cyclically.

It appeared, mathematically, that the value of the planet's gravitational acceleration would put an upper limit on the rate of travel possible by this means. The agent found himself a little dubious about the engineering advantages of it. If one had to travel on the surface, wheels seemed easier—although an irregular surface might present further difficulties. Few Conservationists, surely, had confronted problems so difficult to resolve.

At least, he had eliminated the last possible doubt that the things were non-metallic, non-electric machines, since he had actually seen them move in a manner that verified and complemented his seismic observations. This implied that the natives were not merely cultured, *but had developed a physical science equal to, perhaps greater, than that of the agent's own race.* The latter was certainly possible, since he had not the faintest idea of what was the operative principle of the devices. It was a disturbing speculation, but he refused to enlarge upon it emotionally. Obviously they had some electrical equipment. The signal detector and broadcasting device, as well as the ionization cylinder, were quite evidently as artificial as his own ship. Their science, regardless of its development, could not be entirely alien. It might be possible for him to learn something about it. If so, it was important that he begin—for the equipment needed to stop the moles would have to be obtained from these people in rather short order.

The agent examined once more, as precisely as his sensory equipment permitted, every detail of the things around him, which were now returning slowly, after their hasty withdrawal. He broadcast his "Hello" again, and carefully noted the way it affected the receiver. When the answer came, he checked with equal care the source of the modulating energy.

The result was interesting. The receiver apparently did not consider the carrier waves important. It damped them out and used, through most of its circuitry, a secondary signal consisting of the original modulations. This was caused to vary the strength of a magnetic field which, as nearly as the agent could tell, was used to impart mechanical motion to an object principally non-metallic.

He could get only a rough idea of its size and shape from the space left for it in the mechanism. The evidence seemed to indicate that the whole device simply rebroadcast the modulation of the original signal mechanically into the atmosphere.

He knew, of course, that a gas *could* carry compression waves, though it had never occurred to him that they might be of any particular use. He had simply never stopped to wonder why his method of digging was more effective on a planet with atmosphere. It did no good to blame oneself for such oversights when the fat was in the fire. Anyway, he was sure of one thing. The waves were being used to carry the signals controlling the machines. Certainly no others were.

They also served for communication, since similar waves appeared to be received by the same disc in the signal device, and were used to modulate its broadcast electromagnetic impulses. This process seemed pointless, except as a means of long-distance communication. Probably pressure waves did not transmit energy so effectively through a gas as electromagnetic radiation carried it through space. So far, so good.

It all tied in, more or less, with the evident fact that these machines were not electrical, even if it did not begin to explain how they actually worked. Some sort of more precise analysis would, of course, be needed. The metal he could detect about the things seemed quite purposeless, and he did not see that it was likely to help.

It was present in small, disconnected bits and was devoid of electrical energy, if you brushed aside the minute currents generated by its motion in the planet's magnetic field.

The machines, then, were made virtually entirely of non-conductors, and should be about as easy for the agent to examine as a device consisting exclusively of gas jets and magnetic fields would be for a human being.

This meant that the analysis would have to be by highly indirect methods. A chemist, with his laboratory machine, might be able to do the job in microseconds. But a traveling device, like the scout ship, had no equipment designed with any such purpose in mind.

He suspected that this was one of the situations where the sensile members of his race—the great majority—would leap at the chance to show their superiority over one who was bound to a machine. It had always been that way. It was a common enough feeling among those whose lives were primarily intellectual. The doers, like the agent, countered it with a clear recognition of the necessity for their work. At the moment, however, the agent rather wished that a normal person had been present, to show his intellectual superiority.

Then he realized that his own possession of machinery did not disqualify him as an intelligent being. If a member of his race could solve this problem, it was as likely to be himself as anyone else. He would have to use all his knowledge, of course, not just the specialized information that was all the millennia of flight demanded.

Enough knowledge should be there. He had, of course, been young when he had elected this life, but he had had much thinking time before his career was actually begun. Also, there had been a good deal of time to think as he drifted among the stars, and opportunities to gather data that planet bound thinkers had never possessed.

He would have to go back to the most elemental principles of thought—if he could. First, he had decided, on the basis of what seemed adequate evidence, that the planet was inhabited—that its inhabitants used machines and, therefore, had freedom of motion—and that these machines were based on a technology almost, but not quite wholly, alien to his own.

Nevertheless, the devices must operate under the same physical laws that obtained elsewhere in the universe. This meant that they must take in some form of energy, must perform a desired action, and must eventually account for the energy as heat.

The energy was not electric or magnetic, since he could have detected the presence of that kind of energy directly. It was not gravitational, since the gravitational potential of these machines—when measured as a function of their distance from the planet's center—had actually increased since he had first detected them. It was barely possible, of course, that some primary source beyond his detection-range might work on such a basis. But for the moment that hardly bothered him. It could be filed away for future reference.

There was almost certainly no direct mechanical link with a distant energy source. He felt sure that he would have seen any such, during his brief trip aloft.

Chemical energy, however, remained a distinct possibility. Normally—which usually meant, he reflected wryly, circumstances in which intelligence had not taken a hand— chemical reactions were too slow to provide useful energy, even though they were responsible for life. However, on a planet infested with such weirdly active carbon compounds, it would not do to be dogmatic on the matter.

It was known that reactions, in such circumstances, did go with enormous speed, though little actual quantitative work had been done on the matter of the energy involved. It was quite conceivable, in any case, that there might be some method of turning chemical directly into mechanical energy, without involving electricity as an intermediate stage.

Looked at from this viewpoint, several more possibilities as to the planet became evident. Its natives could survive, either by nature or intelligent adaptation, in an oxygen-rich atmosphere. Oxygen was one of the most virulently active elements in existence. Hence, it might not be too surprising to find such a people developing a chemical technology and bypassing the electricity a living creature should logically use—but wait. They had *not* bypassed electricity.

There were auxiliary machines, among the vehicles facing him, which did use it. Perhaps, these people had originally developed a normal technology, but, for some unaccountable reason, had never mastered space flight! That was more than likely, if one assumed they did not merely tolerate oxygen, but *needed* it.

In that case, they would inevitably exhaust, in a relatively short time, the metal resources of a single planet.

They would be faced with the choice of developing machines that did not make demands on the metal supply, or of sinking to barbarism during the millions of years it would take new metal deposits to concentrate to usability.

This race might have succeeded in accomplishing the former—in which case, the exhaustion of the local ore veins could not be blamed on the poachers after all. The marauder might have planted the torpedoes in momentary pique, believing that a regular freighter had been there first and hoping to throw the production schedule of this planet out of step with that which had been recorded for it.

It was a very attractive idea, but the agent decided he should not go quite so far in pure speculation. There should be other possible sources of energy besides chemical activity, promising as such energy appeared to be. He could, for example, detect a pressure against his hull, which seemed to be due to currents in the atmosphere. These must necessarily carry energy, though it seemed, at first estimate, that it could hardly be quantitatively adequate to run these machines.

There was nuclear energy. Obviously, these aliens did not use it directly, yet the possibility remained that it was their primary source and was stored in some non-self-destructive form within them. Strength was lent to this possibility by the presence of the ionization tube, which might well be used to locate radioactive materials. If, of course, the normal senses of the creatures were inadequate for the task. Atomic energy not under rigid control was always a rather frightening thing to contemplate, and he did not dwell on certain other unlikely possibilities concerning it.

He had already thought of solar energy, but had seen nothing to offset any of his earlier objections to this theory. On the whole, the chemical idea seemed the most worth following up.

He searched his memory for the little he knew about the high-speed chemical reactions of free oxygen environments, and found a few helpful items. For one, they did involve solar energy—they employed it usually in breaking down water. The oxygen was freed to the surroundings, and the hydrogen combined with oxides of carbon to produce carbohydrates.

These, in turn, could react upon each other, with simple compounds and with some of the free oxygen, to produce incredibly complex substances whose detailed structure had never been worked out by any chemist of his people. This situation should, of course, result in a continual increase of free oxygen in the planet's atmosphere at the expense of the water.

Observation indicated that, actually, an equilibrium was usually attained in this respect. Whether the oxygen re-combined spontaneously with the hydrogen in the compounds, or whether still other high-speed reactions, of the same general type as the photosynthetic ones, did the trick, was still a matter of debate. Even the agent could understand, however, that the combination of oxygen with almost any of the complex carbon-hydrogen compounds would return the energy originally supplied by the sun.

If the compounds had any reasonable density, it should be possible to store quite a fuel supply in a very small space that way, using atmospheric oxygen to combine with it whenever desired. Even without precise figures, he felt sure that this would constitute an adequate energy-source for the machines he had been watching.

Was there anything he had overlooked? No—he was nothing if not thorough when he undertook a task of objective scientific analysis. A doer had his own pride to safeguard, and if he was not an intellectual in a strict sense, he did possess a first-rate mind.

How could this theory be checked experimentally? If it proved correct, there should be, somewhere on or within these machines, a store of hydrogen-carbon compounds. They should be absorbing atmospheric oxygen at a fairly high rate. And they should be exhausting water and, possibly, oxides of carbon.

He had no means for recognizing the hydrogen-carbon compounds, even if he found them, so there seemed little point in trying to take one of the mechanisms apart. No point even if its operator proved willing to allow it. However, there seemed to be a possible way of attacking the problem through the other facts. If an oxidizing reaction of the sort he had envisioned went on in a confined space, what would happen to the pressure? He pondered the problem.

Producing solid oxides would reduce pressure by removing oxygen. The formation of carbon dioxide would leave it unchanged, for there would be the same number of molecules after the reaction as before. Making water or carbon monoxide would give a pressure increase, since each molecule of oxygen would go into two molecules of the product.

All this, of course, assumed that water and the oxides of carbon were gases at this temperature. The method offered him two out of three chances of learning something—better, really, since it was likely that two, or all three, of the reactions occurred together. Only if CO_2 alone were produced, would there be a negative result. The catch seemed to be how one was to seal one of these devices in a gas-tight container, with a limited amount of atmosphere?

The container, of course, was available. His own ship had a good deal of waste space, left deliberately to allow for later modifications, if and when they were developed. He could open his hull for maintenance at virtually any point, and the openings were naturally designed to seal gas-tight, since his occupation was more than likely to lead him into corrosive atmospheres such as this.

He would have to be sure that he let the planet's air only into chambers where it could not reach either his own tissues or the ship's circuitry. No, wait. The test should take only minutes or hours, not years. Both his flesh and the silver wires could stand oxygen that long, and he could get rid of it later by opening the hull to the vacuum of space. That made matters easier—much easier.

But how could he detect the change in pressure, if it did occur? He did have manometers, of course. But they were vented to the outside of his hull. No one had foreseen a need for measuring internal pressure. He would have to do some more hard thinking.

What effects would pressure produce, besides merely mechanical ones? There would not be enough change, in the electrical properties of the exposed wires, for even the agent to detect. The change would probably not be fast enough to alter the temperature noticeably. And even if it did alter it, he would not be able to tell whether the change were due to gas laws, or simply the operation of the machine.

In the temperature range of this world, it was not really certain that all the products were gaseous, anyway. The mere fact that he had detected them in that form, during his approach, meant nothing. The infrared spectrographic equipment he had used would have picked up trace quantities. It was unfortunate that its receivers were also aimed outward.

The agent could not, for the life of him, recall the vapor-pressure curves of any of the expected products—though, come to think of it, *something* was liquid here. The clouds he could see proved that, as did their precipitation on his half. He could not assume that it was one of the products he sought, however, and his best bet was still to maintain pressure change. If he could do it...

CHAPTER EIGHT

STUNNED AND SHAKEN, the three humans stared at the star-traveler, which had now so unbelievably and unexpectedly revealed itself in full. And the star-traveler stared back at them through its dull, opaque vision windows.

It was Candace Parsons who spoke first. "Why!" she exclaimed in a strained, oddly small voice. "Why—it looks like a gigantic bathysphere! Maybe..." she fell silent.

Hal Parsons, ignoring the rain that streamed down his face, said, "Maybe what, baby?"

"I don't know." Candace's voice remained off-pitch, tremulous. "I guess I was thinking that maybe—if he is from outer space—our atmosphere is like an ocean to him. Maybe he is a bathysphere."

"Why do you refer to that thing as *he?*" her husband asked sharply. "Whatever is inside probably has no more concept of sex as we know it than an amoeba."

"I don't know. I really don't know, Hal." Candace mopped the rainwater from her face with a khaki towel she had brought from the jeep. "I don't know, but *he*—just *seems* masculine somehow."

"If that's a bathysphere," put in Truck MacLaurie, with a forced attempt at levity, "I'd surer than hell hate to take a bath in it. How would I ever get out?"

"Truck!" said Candace, biting her under-lip. "Don't you honestly know what a bathysphere is?"

"Isn't it a round bathtub?" Truck asked.

"For your information," Candace said, more to herself than to the young man who had blundered, "A bathysphere is a globular device designed by William Beebe for deep

158

underwater observation.   Professor Piccard later used an improved model to—"

Her husband, who kept his eyes riveted on the alien visitor, suddenly leapt at her and pushed her flat on her face against the hillside. As he did so he yelled at Truck, *"For God's sake, flatten out!"*

The alien was on the move.

There could be no doubt about it this time. Candace, her face ashen, felt the near-earthquake vibration emanating from the advancing sphere and looked up, barely in time to see it zoom skyward, leaving boiling earth and mud in its wake.

The alien's rise was as rapid as the pursuit-foiling lifting processes attributed to flying saucers in the nation's press. He shot up a thousand feet—two thousand—and again they smelled the acrid aroma of metal heating up unbearably from friction with the atmosphere.

Feeling a sudden, shocking, incongruous disappointment, Candace cried, "Oh—he's getting away! *He's leaving Earth."*

"No he isn't," said Truck, staring grimly up into the rain. "Get a load of that!"

That proved to be a sudden lateral maneuver on the part of the alien. It moved several hundred yards sideways and again was immobile. It was apparently as capable of remaining immobile in the atmosphere as it had been immediately following its self-burial in the rocky soil.

Candace could see the great round eyes, reduced to mere dots in the distance, trained steadily upon the three of them. She experienced paralyzing fear. It was obvious now that the alien failed to welcome close contact with humans, and was determined to resist investigation.

Secondarily—but no less frightening—was the thought that, being an alien, it could scarcely be expected to have humanitarian sympathies. It would probably be no more hesitant about wiping them out than most people were about destroying bothersome insects.

She glanced at her husband for reassurance, but saw in his fear-shadowed, eyes a reflection of her own fears. She had learned, long ago—in high-school biology—that the legend of a snake's ability to paralyze a bird-victim with an hypnotic stare was utterly false. Yet Hal's trapped gaze failed to refute that ancient tale. His eyes remained fixed upon the strange object hovering almost motionless above them, half-veiled by a mist of its own creation.

Then, suddenly, Candace screamed. The alien was returning, swooping directly down toward them with the speed of a V-2. Before the echoes of her scream could dwindle and die away, it had landed—not upon them but in its former resting-place. It perched there lightly, dominating the immediate landscape, its opaque twin lenses still fixed implacably upon them.

It was Harold, lifting himself slowly from the rain-soaked ground, who said, "Now I wonder just what in hell was the precise purpose of that maneuver."

Candace, close to hysteria from the backlash of terror and shock, replied, "You might just as well ask why such a creature does anything?"

"Funny thing," said Truck, brushing mud from the front of his clothing. "I think it wanted a better look at us. Did you notice the way it kept those fish-eyes on us all the time it was dancing that rock-and-roll over us?"

"I noticed," Harold Parsons replied tersely, his face still drained of its natural color. "What beats me is why it had to hop around like that."

Truck frowned at the looming bulk of the alien. Then he looked at his companions and rubbed the bristles on his chin. "Funny thing," he repeated. "I'm completely sure now it wasn't trying to scare us."

"Then just what do you think it was trying to do?"

Candace asked.

Truck had latched on to something and, bulldog-like, he was not giving it up. "This probably won't make much sense to you eggheads," he told them, in his southwestern drawl. "But the way that thing acted reminded me of an uncle of mine. His eyes aren't as good as they used to be, and he won't wear bifocals. When he wants a good look at anything close-up, he has to pull his head back. Do you know what I mean?"

"If your uncle looks like that," said Candace, with a tremulous nod at the alien, "it's no wonder you're having trouble with your credits."

"Hold it, baby," said Hal, regarding MacLaurie with something like awe. "I think he's got something. Take a good look at those things our friend sees with—if seeing is what they're for. Its eyes are set at much too flat a curvature to enable it to see anything small and close up without some sort of focusing agent. I can detect no evidence of its having any. In that case..." He paused.

"You mean, I'm right?" Truck asked incredulously.

"I mean you could be," said Parsons. "Nice going, Truck."

He looked thoughtful for a moment, and then he added, "If it really is a space-traveling machine of some sort—and the evidence to date makes that highly probable—then its eyes would be designed for judging objects of immense size, immense distances away. It would need no focusing devices."

"All right, you two geniuses," said Candace, who had recovered a small measure of her equilibrium, "if it really is a space-traveler, why would it have to resort to such extremes just to get a good look at us? Surely it has all kinds of other senses—or instruments for measurement. If not, how could it have gotten here in the first place?"

Harold Parsons fished a limp cigarette from an equally limp pack in his breast pocket. He eyed it in disgust and quickly tossed it away. "Has it occurred to you, baby, that it may not be that simple?" he asked. "If its vision equipment is so faulty under Earth conditions, it undoubtedly is faced with other problems."

He paused, wiped his forehead briefly dry, and added, "I'll stake my Ph.D. that we're just as big a problem to our friend as he is to us. We know that it is capable of radio communication by voice. But, so far, all that it has been able to communicate is the fact that it can indulge in parrot-like mockery of our speech."

"Hey!" said Truck, who had been listening attentively. "You mean it hasn't made sense out of what we were saying."

"What do you think?" said Parsons.

Candace said, "You know, this may be silly, but it makes me think of a movie I saw once—one in which an explorer on a strange island had to learn to get on with the natives by pointing out objects and then repeating over and over their speech equivalents. The natives had to do the same thing."

"You saw it once? I saw it six times," said Truck. "The guy kept pointing at trees and rocks, and describing them in English."

Hal Parsons threw the pack after his discarded cigarette. "Probably it was Robinson Crusoe!" he exploded. "But, once again, Truck, you and Candace could be on the nose. The only trouble is—I don't believe we managed to impart much information while our pal was zooming about." He paused, adding with a frown, "There's only one way to find out."

They plodded back to the jeep. Truck cranked the battery, while Parsons got the radio transmitter into operation. This time, he didn't have to speak first. The moment the receiver was working, he could hear his own voice coming through the earphones in a reiterated, "Who's that? *Hello!...* Who's that? *Hello?"*

Parsons acknowledged, with, "Hello out there. We were watching you just now."

Back it came. "Hello out there. We were watching you just now."

Infuriatingly, frustratingly, it went on—meaningless repetition following meaningless repetition. Finally, as before, Parsons had to give it up in disgust.

Candace produced some dry cigarettes from the expedition stores, and she and Hal smoked them silently, under the shelter of the jeep-top. Truck, who was in training, did not join them. It was a damp, disheartening breathing spell.

Finally, Candace said, "Well, remember Valley Forge. It's always darkest before the dawn."

"Frankly, I'd rather not think about Valley Forge right now," said Parsons unhappily. "If that thing isn't able to make sense out of us unless it sees us, and it can't see us—how in hell are we going to make sense out of it? I think we'd better get help from outside—if we can. Okay, it's uphill for us again."

"Maybe not," said Truck. "Listen."

They heard the faint thrum of plane engines coming through the overcast, maintaining itself, growing louder. Parsons threw his cigarette away and said, "Come on, Truck. Let's get going."

It was the general again, anxious to know how they were making out. Parsons told him in terse syllables. Truck looked up from his battery-duty and said, "Getting anywhere, Sergeant?" And was rewarded by a shut-your-mouth gesture.

Parsons said, "I know it's tough. But you must be able to get through to us somehow. How about dropping a couple of philologists by 'chute?"

"We may have to," was the reply. "But only as a last resort. Blast this rain! But you're doing okay, Professor. Stay with it."

And that was that. It was a gloomy threesome that made its way slowly over the soggy hillside from jeep to alien. They walked slowly around the alien, and then stood in front of it, regarding a little more calmly now the disc-like, too-flat lenses that had gone opaque again.

"I wonder if it can see us at all from this distance," Parsons mused. Then, irrelevantly, "You wouldn't think, with all the resources of modern science and the Air Force, they'd let a little rain stop them cold."

"It isn't a *little* rain," said Candace, who had been listening to her husband's colloquy with the general through one earphone. "It's a lot of rain—and it has raised hob all around here. The soil and rock formations aren't used to so much moisture. They just can't take it."

"Let's hope we can take it a while longer," said Parsons, putting an arm around her and squeezing.

"Don't, honey," she said. "I just can't take it right now."

"Hey!" called Truck, who'd been eyeing the monster from a bit to one side. "Watch it! Something's happening—"

CHAPTER NINE

As usual, the solution was ridiculously simple, once the traveler had thought of it. Most of the access-doors in the hull opened outward and all were operated electrically. He had perfect control over the current supplied to their operating motors. He knew that if he refrained from latching one or more of the doors, and simply held it shut with the motor, he could sense directly the amount of effort needed to keep it sealed against the internal pressure.

As far as he was concerned, it was a quantitative solution—if the pressure increased. If it decreased—well, he would know it, from the extra effort needed to open the door. He was concentrating on immediate small details now—and very wisely.

With his machine, action could follow thought without delay. The moment he had his answer, a door swung open in the side of the great metal egg he was driving, and Earth's air poured in. Good as his seals were, the ship had not, of course, retained any significant amount of gas in the millennia it had been in space.

He did not bother to develop a plan for enticing one of the machines through the opening. He assumed, quite justly, that any intelligent mind must have a fair proportion of curiosity in its makeup. The fact that self-preservation might oppose this influence did not, as far as the agent knew or suspect, apply to the present situation. The risk of sacrificing even an expensive remote-controlled machine should be well worth taking in such circumstances. He simply waited for one of the devices to be driven into his ship.

Before this happened, however, there was a good deal of

conversation among the machines present and, he presumed, the distant broadcaster—if, of course, it could be called conversation. The agent was still unable to reconcile this supposition with the absence of intelligent life in the present group.

At last, however, the expected event occurred. One of the machines swung about and moved toward the opening in the hull. Just outside, it halted, and the agent guessed at a brief burst of atmospheric pressure waves, though his manometers did not react fast enough to catch them. It was then that it entered.

It traveled on four struts instead of two. It became completely horizontal and advanced on the supporting struts. Evidently the upper ones, which the agent had seen, could be used for locomotion when desirable. Its entrance was slower than by its usual rate of motion, though the agent could not imagine why. The suggestion that slower motion made detail observation easier would never have occurred to a being whose perception and recording operations occupied fractions of a microsecond. Whatever the reason for the delay, it finally managed to get inside.

The agent wasted no time. Ready to observe anything and everything that resulted, he shut the access hatch.

Results, by his reaction-time standards, were slow—additional evidence that remote control was involved. The electromagnetic unit burst into activity the instant things finally began to happen. Some of the machines outside began to tap on the hull with dimly perceptible solid fragments, apparently pieces of silicate rock. The agent tried to find regularities in the blows that might be interpreted as communication code of some sort. He failed.

One of the devices, standing a little distance away, moved one of its attached fragments of metal until a hollow cylinder—which formed part of it—was in line with the hull.

After a long moment the more distant end of the cylinder filled with gas, sufficiently ionized to be clearly perceptible to the alien.

The gas must have been under considerable pressure, for almost instantly it began to expand, driving before it a smaller fragment of metal that had plugged the tube. This fragment became progressively easier to perceive as its speed through the planet's magnetic field increased.

It emerged from the near end of the cylinder with sufficient momentum to continue in a nearly linear course, until it made contact with the hull. The agent watched with mounting excitement as it flattened, spread out and finally broke into many pieces. Incredible! He analyzed it, both electrically and mechanically, from the way it broke up. But he could make no sense of the operation.

After a time, the pounding ceased, and the two machines remaining outside drew together. No obvious activity came from them for some time.

Inside the hull, more interesting, possibly more understandable, events were taking place. The moment the door had closed, the machine trapped within had attempted to withdraw. Its action was a trifle faster than that of the ones still outside. The agent could not decide whether this meant that the escape reaction was automatic, or that a distant controller had turned his attention to the captive machine first.

It had pounded aggressively on the inside of the door in the same seemingly plan-less fashion as its fellows. Then it had slowed down, and began to move another of the strangely fashioned pieces of metal distributed about its frame. This abruptly became clearly perceptible, as an electric current began to flow through portions of its structure.

The source of the current was a seemingly endless supply of metallic ions—quite evidently chemical energy could be used for something. The current's function was less obvious, since it was led through a conductor whose greatest resistance was concentrated in a tight metal spiral.

This must in some way have been shielded from atmospheric oxygen, since, while it must have reached a fairly high temperature if the ion cloud around it meant anything, it nevertheless remained uncorroded. Heating the wire seemed all that the device accomplished—the agent refused to believe that the ion cloud was intense enough to help either in action or perception. The light and heat radiated were inconsiderable, but—wait! Perhaps that was it—perhaps *this* machine had eyes!

The agent examined the electrical device more closely, and discovered that part of its uncharged structure consisted of a roughly paraboloidal piece of metal, which must certainly have been able to focus light into a beam of sorts.

A few moments later, it became evident that it did just that. The agent's body was exposed in several places in this part of the ship, and time after time one part would be struck by radiance, while the rest were in more or less complete darkness. Furthermore, a few minutes' observation showed that when the machine moved at all it followed the direction in which the light beam happened to be pointing at the time.

Sometimes it did not move, though the beam kept roving around the chamber. The agent deduced from that one of two things. Either the device had several eyes, or the one it had was movable over virtually the entire sphere of possible directions. The thing was making an orderly survey of the interior of the space in which it was trapped. But it was carefully refraining from touching anything except the floor on which it stood.

That portions of this floor consisted of the agent's tissue made no difference to either party—as far as either knew. But the agent began to wonder how much of the exposed machinery of the ship would be comprehensible to the presumed distant observer.

Still more, he wondered how this presumed observer maintained contact with his machine. There was no energy whatever—in any form that the agent could detect—getting through his hull, either to or from the trapped machine. A minor exception to this might be the pressure waves generated by the stones striking his hull. But he had already failed to find in these blows any pattern at all, much less one which could be correlated with the actions of the machine inside.

Naturally, the thought that this might be an automatic device, similar to the mole robots, could hardly help occurring to the Conservationist. If this were the case, its present behavior was far more complicated than that of any such machine he had ever encountered. But hold on—he had already faced the implications inherent in that idea. So the technology of this world was more advanced, in some ways, than his own. There were still things the natives didn't know—things which would most certainly hurt them. Any concern he might have felt about himself was drowned in this larger solicitude.

He wondered whether he could so operate any of his own machinery to or through his prisoner, so as to convey a message of any sort. Certainly, if it used light as a vehicle of perception, it could detect motion on the part of the relays. For example—they were larger by quite a margin than the wavelength of the radiation the hot wire was emitting in greatest strength.

There were several hundred thousand of them in the dozen square yards exposed to the direct-line vision of the captive, which should be enough to form some sort of pattern. Some sort of pattern, that is, if their owner could figure out how to operate them without making the ship misbehave.

He was still pondering this problem, along with the question of just what would be a meaningful pattern to the operators of the machine, when his attention was once more drawn to the outside.

The machines there seemed to have taken up a definite course of action. They had once more approached the hull, and were doing something to it that he could not at first quite understand. It quickly enough became evident, however. The brightness of the images he was receiving through the eyes, to which he had naturally been paying very little attention, began rapidly to decrease.

Within a minute or so, the lenses ceased to transmit at all.

His tactile "sense" consisted in part of the ability to analyze the response of his hull to the vibrating impulses he applied to it. If such impulses were followed faithfully he could be sure that there was no mass in contact with the surface. On the other hand, if they were damped to any extent, he could form a fairly accurate idea of the amount and even some of the physical properties of such a mass.

In the present case, he discovered almost instantly that his eye lenses had been covered with a most peculiar substance. It not only adhered tenaciously to them, but seemed to absorb without noticeable reaction the same vibrations that had sent the soil dancing out of his way like summer chaff in a breeze. This did not particularly bother him, since the eyes were nearly useless for watching the machines anyway. But he kept trying to shake the material off, while he considered the implications of the move.

One was that the machines depended, far more heavily than he had suspected, on the sense of sight, and must suppose that he did likewise. Another was that they were about to take measures that they did not want observed by him. He did not worry seriously about anything they could do to his ship, but he began to listen very carefully for their footsteps all the same.

Another possibility was that they simply did not want him to flyaway with the captive machine. To a race dependent upon sight, no doubt the idea of flying without it was unthinkable. He wondered, fleetingly, whether he should move a few hundred yards, just to see what effect the act had on them. Then the actions they were already performing caught his attention, and he shelved the notion. He became alarmed at what appeared to be an abrupt change of plan.

Two of the things were leaving the neighborhood, in a direction more or less toward the other electromagnetic radiator. Making allowances for the difficulty these machines apparently suffered in traveling over uneven terrain, the agent felt reasonably sure that this was their goal. The other two remained near him and settled down to relative motionlessness, as nearly as he could tell. He comforted himself with the thought that whatever plan they were attempting might demand some time to mature.

Perhaps the departing machines were going after additional equipment, though it appeared their goal might be attained more rapidly by sending other machines from the control point. However, it was quite possible that no others were available—such was likely enough to be the case on any of his own worlds, where only one individual in five hundred was machine-equipped, and over half of these were incapable of locomotion. Pride swelled in him at the thought, but he dismissed it as unworthy.

His soliloquy was interrupted by something that had not happened to him since his ship had first lifted from the world on which it had been built. The incident itself was minor, but its implications were not. The hull vibration, which he was still applying near all of his aboveground eyes, *stopped* near one of them.

He had not stopped it. The command for the carefully planned motion pattern was still flowing along his nerves. It should have been inducing the appropriate response in a fairly large group of relays. Something had gone wrong, and it produced a sudden crisis in his thinking.

The ship, of course, was equipped with a fantastic number of test-circuits, and he began to use them for all they were worth. It took him about three milliseconds to learn a significant fact. All the inoperative relays were close to, or actually within, the compartment where the captive machine was located. Closer checking showed that the trouble was mechanical—the tiny switches were being held in whatever position they had been in when the trouble struck.

Worse, the paralysis was spreading. It was spreading with a terrifying rapidity. The basic cause was not hard to guess, even with the details far from obvious. The agent instantly unsealed the door barring his captive from the outside world, and felt thankful that the controls involved still functioned.

The thing lost no time in getting out, and the pilot lost even less in getting the door securely sealed after it. For the time being, he completely ignored what went on outside, while he strove to remedy the weird disability. He was far from consoled by the thought, when it struck him, that he had proved what he wanted to know.

Something solid had blocked the relays—had, more accurately, *formed around* their microscopic moving parts. Whatever it was must have come in gas form for he would have felt the localized weight of a liquid, even inside. Most of the interior of his ship, as well as his own flesh, was still far colder than the planet on which he was lying.

Quite evidently one of the exhaust products of the captive machine, released as a gas, had frozen wherever it touched a cold surface. It might have been either water or one of the oxides of carbon. The agent neither knew nor cared. He proceeded to run as much current as possible through all his test-circuits, with the object of creating enough resistance-heat to evaporate the material.

The process took long enough to make him doubt seriously that his conclusion could be correct. But eventually the frozen relays began to come back into service. He could have speeded up the process, by going up a few miles and exposing his interior to the lowered pressure, and he knew enough physics to be aware of the fact.

It spoke strongly for the shock he had received that he never thought of this until evaporation was nearly complete. It was lucky for his peace of mind that he never realized what the liquid water—formed in the process—might have done to his circuits. Fortunately, formed as it had been, it contained virtually no dissolved electrolytes and caused no shorts.

He realized, suddenly, that he had permitted his attention to stray from the doings of the nearby machines for what might be an unwise length of time, and at once resumed his listening. Apparently, they were still doing nothing. No seismic impulses were originating in the area where he had last perceived them. That eased his mind a trifle, and he returned to the problem of the material covering his eyes.

This stuff seemed to be changing slightly in its properties. Its elasticity was increasing, for one thing, and the change seemed to be taking place more rapidly on the side from which the air currents were coming. The agent could think of no explanation for this. He tried differing vibration patterns on the stuff, manipulating them with the skill of an artist—but a long time passed before he had anything approaching success.

At last, however, a minute flake of the material cracked free and fell away—*and he could really see! He could actually make out what was going on!*

CHAPTER TEN

To UNDERSTAND what had gone on outside the alien to cause all this on a purely human plane, an observer of the whole would have had to go back to an earlier event entirely of Truck's doing.

As Truck spoke, something very definitely was happening to the visitor from outer space. Following the young athlete's pointing forefinger, the Parsons saw, with astonishment, that a section of the globular metal body was slowly, steadily opening—or was being opened.

It was circular, perhaps two feet in diameter, and its opening looked unexpectedly simple for a creature, or a machine, capable of interstellar flight. A section of the full, or outer body simply dropped open and outward—apparently on hinges.

"Like dropped underwear," Candace murmured, to be instantly quelled by a severely reproving look from her husband.

His expression remained firm.

"I know what you're thinking," he told her. "It seems too simple. But consider this. Any alien using such a device on a strange world must be damned well capable of protecting itself."

"Maybe it's an airlock," suggested Truck.

"Maybe," said Hal Parsons, "but don't bet on it. It could be anything. We don't know enough about the nature of this—" He stopped, as Candace clutched his sleeve. "What is it, baby?" he demanded.

"Hal honey," she said, panic returning to envelop her like a torrent of water far colder than the rain. "Hal, honey, do you suppose it's coming out?"

"*It!*" Truck suggested. "Why not *them*. Why not some of those little green men that fly-boy was talking about."

Parsons stared apprehensively at the opening in an effort to penetrate the darkness within. But he could see nothing— not even a shadow advancing toward them or hovering motionless in the gloom. He looked oddly at Truck and then began to lead his wife toward the jeep.

"Come on, Candace," he said. "We'd better get the rifle from the trailer—just in case."

For an instant, Candace hesitated. She was a self-reliant, wholly modern girl, proud of her ability to handle herself as well as any man, in almost any situation. But her self-reliance crumbled when she looked again at the alien—huge, globular, impervious—with the ominous, gaping door part way up one of its flanks. This, obviously, was not a situation to be handled with reckless assurance.

She said, "Okay, honey," in a very meek voice.

Parsons said, "Better stick with us, Truck."

"I want to see what's going on," said MacLaurie, in his easy drawl. "Anyway, I don't figure our little pal here means any harm."

"Just how do you figure that?" Parsons asked sharply.

"If it was going to hurt us, it would have done so long before this," was Truck's sage reply.

"Don't be foolish, Truck," said Candace in an urgent tone. "It may have been merely softening us up before it opened that door."

Truck silenced her with, "I've a hunch you've been reading too many science-fiction stories lately, Candace."

"Hold tight then until we get back," Hal commanded. To his wife, in a lower voice he said, "I don't like leaving him here, either. But his mind's made up, and someone had better keep an eye on it."

"If that's *all* he does," murmured Candace.

"What's that?" her husband demanded. "What do you mean?"

"Nothing, honey," she said. But so great was her concern that she glanced several times over her shoulder while en route to the trailer. Fortunately for her peace of mind each time she looked the situation remained unchanged. Truck still stood there, his hands at his waist, his head cocked a little on one side as he regarded the menacing wide-open door.

"Better hurry, honey," she urged as they neared the jeep. "Something we can't cope with may happen any moment now!"

"So far, damn little has happened," grunted Parsons. "I'm beginning to wish it *would* do something menacing. This stalemate is getting on my nerves."

"I'm not so much worried about what it may do," said Candace. "At least, not right now. It's what Truck may do that's got me frightened."

Hal looked at her skeptically. But he speeded up his motions nevertheless. He got the canvas-covered Winchester out from under the trailer tarpaulin, stuffed a box of bullets into pants' pocket and began hurrying back towards the hillside almost at a run.

They were two-thirds of the way towards their destination when Candace, tagging and slipping a little at his heels, again gripped his arm convulsively and said, "Hal, he's going to do it. He's going inside!"

Parsons stopped dead in his tracks and yelled, "Truck! Stay where you are! Do you hear me? Don't go any nearer until we get there!"

As they watched, appalled, Truck MacLaurie looked over his shoulder at them. For a moment his grin flashed in the rain. Then moving with a deliberation that masked the speed he was employing—a trick his opponents on the football field had learned to rue, he moved directly toward the round, open door in the alien's flank, hoisted himself up to it, wriggled a moment or two and vanished inside.

A moment later, his deep voice rumbled at them through the rain. "I'm all right!" he shouted. "Don't worry!"

It was then that, without sound or warning, the open door in the alien's flank swung shut, sealing Truck inside.

Hal and Candace exchanged appalled glances and began to run toward the ship. Candace sprinted, stumbling and gasping, directly toward it. She would have hammered on the alien metal barrier with her fists had Hal not restrained her.

"Easy," he said in tones that suggested calmness maintained only by the greatest effort. "Easy, baby. There's no sense of all of us walking into a trap until we see what can be done."

"But I can hear him!" she cried. And at that moment audible sounds of something banging on the inside of the alien trap could be heard.

"Hold it, honey," said Hal. He continued to restrain her until, finally, she gave up, her face white with horror beneath the mud that caked it. Then he picked up a couple of loose stones and fired them, hard, one after the other at the portion of the hull where the door had opened.

"I tried to tell you we shouldn't have left him," she burst out, looking wildly around for some stones to throw herself. "Honey, we're responsible for him. We should have made him come with us."

"It's a little late for that now," said Parsons, breathing heavily as he let fly with another stone.

Inside the alien ship, Hal felt for a moment like a soft-bodied larval insect cruelly encased in a metallic cocoon. The impulse that had moved him to enter the door had been irresistible. It had occurred to him, even before the Parsons had given him his opportunity, that if an alien ship offering such an invitation took off unvisited he would regret it for the rest of his life.

More than anything else he was motivated by the thought of what a certain little red-headed coed back on the Montana Mines campus might have to say about it. Competition was heavy where that girl was concerned—and as far as Truck could see at the moment, running second would make life insupportable.

He had tried to remind himself of both the danger and idiocy of disobeying Parsons' warning. But—and this was true even with professors—Truck seldom troubled himself with the various levels of college teacherdom. Parsons, to Truck, was like most faculty members, tending to be overcautious about almost everything. A fine character, but too damned careful.

The door had been there, Truck was there—and the result had been as inevitable as Candace had foreseen. What Truck hadn't figured on was that his host would elect to slam the door on him so quickly.

Inside, it was dark—and it was cold. It was cold with a bone-chilling, impersonal quality that reminded the gladiator of the storage room in the Arizona meatpacking establishment where he'd held a summer job two seasons back. For one horrible moment he had the ghastly idea that he was undergoing some sort of deep freeze process, following which he would be taken back to his chilly host's home planet, for thawing out and laboratory dissection.

A saving memory reminded him that, minutes earlier, he had ribbed Candace unmercifully about her having read too many science fiction magazines. Now, it appeared, the proverbial shoe was on the other foot with a vengeance—his own size thirteen. She might have read too many such stories, but he was living too many—one too many, to be exact.

But the vagrant whimsy restored what had become rather a shaky sanity—and a sane Truck MacLaurie, while not exactly a mental giant, was capable in an emergency of formidable thought and action. He realized that his surroundings, while unpleasantly cold, were not of a sufficiently low temperature to quick-freeze him. The process would last a long time. It might be unpleasant, but it offered further possibilities of escape.

He wondered what his surroundings looked like, and instantly remembered that he had stuffed a flashlight into his pants' pocket that very morning, in case he had to work the radio battery entirely under the jeep tarpaulin—to keep it from getting wet. In two seconds he had the flash out and turned on, and was surveying the strange cell in which he appeared to be imprisoned.

Earlier that year, one of his roommates, who was something of an electrical handyman, had taken apart an ailing television set in his fraternity house. Truck's brief glimpse of the seemingly endless and incomprehensible confusion of wires, in their pink insulation wrappers, had conjured up a vision of a beehive being invaded by an army of pink worms.

Now he derived somewhat the same impression—save that the worms appeared to be of white metal, either silver or platinum, and the confusion even greater. He bent over a sector of the complex wiring that looked vaguely familiar, then jumped as a thump sounded from outside the hull. It was quickly followed by another thump.

Good old Doc! he thought, and hammered back until his hand began to ache. He considered using the flashlight, then decided against it. The thumping stopped, and he wondered how Jonah had felt in the whale's belly, without even a flashlight.

Better keep moving, he told himself, as he felt the gooseflesh form on his forearms. *Better keep looking around. Better keep trying to make this whale sick enough to throw me up...*

Outside, Hal and Candace Parsons were engaged in grim activity, as Hal prepared to see what effect the rifle would have. "It won't do much good," he said somberly, slipping a bullet into the chamber. "I was figuring on using it more against what came out, if necessary, than against that solid beryllium egg, or whatever it is."

"Maybe you'd better not shoot," said Candace. "You might make it do something drastic. You might make it kill Truck, or take off with him."

"On the other hand," Hal said, trying to sight against one of the invisible hinges of the round trapdoor in its flank, "I don't think I can hurt him much. But I just might annoy him into reopening that damned porthole."

He pulled the trigger, and they looked on, a bit desperately, as the steel-jacketed slug was shattered against the impervious hull. Somewhat to their relief, nothing happened. But there were no more thumps from inside the big globe.

"We've got to get help," said Hal quietly, returning the rifle to its canvas cover, before it could be damaged by the rain. "This situation has got out of hand. I don't care how many scientists break their skulls when they drop them through the cloud layer. We can't stand by and leave Truck trapped in there."

"Of course we can't," said Candace. "I'm glad you feel so strongly about it. I was afraid he was getting on your nerves."

"Of course he was getting on my nerves," Hal Parsons said, somewhat testily. "But that doesn't mean I don't like the ham-handed..." He paused, finished casing the rifle, and added tersely. "Come on—let's get moving. Before we do, let's make sure our pal's eyes—if they *are* eyes—can't see what we're doing."

"How do you blindfold a giant baseball?" Candace asked.

"With whatever I can find at hand," said her husband. "You throw a pretty good stone. Let's see how you are at throwing mud."

He showed her what he had in mind, and there was plenty of mud in a hollow of the hillside that had been turned into a small muck-hole by the alien-induced deluge. It took them about five minutes before the "front" of the alien was well plastered, as well as its "eyes." When the job was done, they moved quickly back toward the jeep and the radio.

"You'll have to crank, baby," he told Candace. "I've been doing the talking to these characters, and there's no sense—"

"Of course." Candace cut him off. "Honey, I'm frightened. Do you suppose that thing has already—?"

She paused, and they both stopped walking. A brash, familiar voice had hailed them from a hundred yards to the rear. Unable to believe their ears, they exchanged a half-fearful glance, and then turned slowly toward the source of the sound. It was Truck, waving and coming toward them at a trot.

"I don't know exactly what happened!" was his answer to the question that burst from them both as he caught up with them. "All of a sudden—just a little while after your shot— he opened the door and I got out of there as fast as I could."

"What was it like?" Candace asked him. "It must have been horrible."

"I dunno," said Truck. "It was sort of interesting—but, brother, was it cold! I damn near froze to death!"

CHAPTER ELEVEN

THE REASON was obvious, of course. With an aperture of thirty centimeters and a focal length of about twenty-seven, the focus of the Conservationist's eye-lenses was highly critical; with the aperture about half a millimeter, as it had been left by the fragment of clay he had broken off, it became a minor matter.

He recognized the machines easily, near the edge of his new field of view, and began to work on the covering of a better-located eye. He did not succeed quite so well here, as the fragment he finally detached was larger, and the image correspondingly less clear, but it was still a good enough job to enable him to follow the actions of the devices visually.

They were not traveling, as he has deduced already. Furthermore, a fourth machine, hitherto unnoticed, had joined them. All four had settled to the ground, so that their main frames took the weight normally carried by the traveling struts, which appeared merely to be propping the roughly cylindrical shapes in a more or less vertical attitude. The different ways in which this was accomplished, in different cases, did not surprise the agent. It would not have occurred to him to expect any two machines to be precisely alike, except perhaps in such standard sub-components as relays. And it was, of course, fortunate that every new development happened in sequence, enabling him to analyze carefully as he went along.

The upper struts were moving rather aimlessly in general, but it did not take long for him to judge that their primary function was manipulation. The objects being handled at the moment were for the most part meaningless—apparently stones, bits of metal without obvious function, utterly unrecognizable objects which might be aggregates of the unfamiliar carbon compounds, though the agent knew no way to prove it. There were one or two exceptions. The device that had projected the slug of metal at his hull was easy to recognize, even though he had not perceived all of it at the time it was being used.

He tried to decide what parts of the machines functioned as their eyes, and was able to find them. It was not difficult, for no other portion was reasonably transparent. He discovered that all these vision organs were now turned toward him, but saw nothing surprising in the fact. The operators must have been familiar with the rest of the landscape, and did not expect anything of interest to show up on it.

Then the traveler noticed that all four of the machines were rising to their struts. As he watched, they began to move toward him.

At the same time, one of them extended a handling member toward a smaller fabrication, which almost immediately turned out to be another electromagnetic radiator. It was put to use at once, being swiftly raised to the upper part of the largest machine in the vicinity of the eyes, while a minor appendage of the handling limb which held it closed a switch.

This started the carrier frequency, after a delay which the agent was able to identify as due to the slow growth of the ion clouds in portions of the apparatus—apparently they were produced by heating metal—and to the inherent lag of mechanical operations. The relays in the device were fantastically huge. They took whole milliseconds to operate and since they rather obviously had components consisting of multi-crystalline pieces of metal, they must have had a sharply limited service life.

Evidently the natives had not gone far enough with metal technology even to get the most out of one world's supplies. This was a side issue, however. A far more interesting development involved the modulation of the carrier. The agent found it possible actually to see the way this was being carried out.

An opening in the machine, not far below the eyes, rimmed with a remarkably flexible substance at whose nature he could only guess, began to open, shut and go through a series of changes of shape. He found it possible to correlate many of these contortions with the modulation of the electromagnetic signal. Apparently the opening was part of a device for generating pressure-wave patterns in the atmosphere.

The agent supposed that whatever plan the distant observers had been maturing must be moving into action, and he wondered what the machines were about to do. He was naturally a little surprised, since he had not expected any developments of this sort so soon.

Then he wondered still more, for the advance toward him, which had been commenced, halted as suddenly as it had begun. Whatever had motivated them had either ceased—or the whole affair was part of an operation whose general nature was still obscure. It would be the better part of valor to assume the latter, he decided.

He watched all four of the machines with minute care. They were now balanced on their support struts. They were neither advancing nor retreating, and the upper members were moving in their usual random fashion. All eyes were still fixed on his ship.

Then he noticed that the pressure-wave assemblies of all four were functioning, although three did not possess any broadcaster whose signal could be modulated. He watched them in fascination. Sometimes—usually, in fact—only one would be generating waves. At others, two, three or all four would be doing so. Even the one with the broadcaster did not always have its main switch closed at such times. Something a little peculiar was definitely occurring.

It had already occurred to the agent that the atmospheric waves carried the control impulses for these machines. Why should the machines themselves be emitting them, however? Receivers should be enough for such machines. Then he recalled another of his passing thoughts, which might serve as an explanation. Perhaps there was only one operator for all of them. And after all, why not? It might be better to think of the whole group as a single machine.

In that case, the pressure waves, traveling among its components, might be coordination signals. They just might be. At any rate, some testing could be done along this line. Whatever limitations he and his ship might have on this world, he could at least set up pressure waves in its atmosphere. Perhaps he could take over actual control of one or more of these assemblies. He had had the idea earlier, in connection with radio waves, and nothing much had come of it. But there seemed no reason not to try it again with sound. Nothing could surpass the experimental method when it was pursued with one strongly likely probability in mind.

A logical pattern to use would be the one that had been broadcast back to the distant observer a few moments before. It had been connected with a fairly simple, definite series of actions, and he had both heard and seen its production. He tried it, causing his hull to move in the complex pattern his memory had recorded a few seconds before. He tried it a second time.

"The thing's howling like a fire siren!"

Just as when he had tried the same test with radio waves, there was no doubt that an effect had been produced, though it was not quite the effect the agent had hoped for. The handling appendages on all four of the things dropped whatever they were holding and snapped toward the upper part of their bodies. Once there, their flattened tips pressed firmly against the sides of the turrets on which their eyes were mounted.

For a moment, none of them produced any waves of its own. Then, the one with the broadcaster began to use it at great length. The agent wondered whether or not to attempt reproduction of the entire pattern it used this time, and decided against it. It was far more likely to be a report than involved in control. He decided to wait and see whether any other action ensued.

What did result might have been foreseen even by one as unfamiliar with mankind as the Conservationist. The machine with the broadcaster began producing more pressure waves, watching the ship as it did so. The agent realized, almost at once, that the controller was also experimenting. He regretted that he could not receive the waves directly, and wondered how he could make the other—or others— understand that their signals should be transmitted electro- magnetically.

As a matter of fact, the agent could have detected the sound waves perfectly well, had it occurred to him to extend one of his seismic receptor-rods into the air. A sound wave carries little energy, and only a minute percentage of that little will pass into a solid from a gas. But an instrument capable of detecting the seismic disturbance set up by a walking man a dozen miles away is not going to be bothered by quantitative problems of that magnitude. However, this fact never dawned on the agent. Yet few would deny that he had done very well.

As it happened, no explanation was necessary for the hidden observer. He must have remembered, fairly quickly, that all the signals the agent had imitated had been radioed, and drawn the obvious conclusion. At any rate, the broadcaster was very shortly pressed into service again. A signal would be transmitted by radio, and the agent would promptly repeat it in sound waves.

Since the Conservationist had not the faintest idea of the significance of any of the signals this was not too helpful—but the native had a way around that. A machine advanced to the hull of the ship and scraped the clay from one of its eyes. The particular eye was the most conveniently located one, to the agent's annoyance. But fortunately it was not the only one through which he could see the things.

Then, an ordered attempt was begun, to provide him with data that would permit him to attach meanings to the various signal groups. Once he had grasped the significance of pointing, matters went merrily on for some time.

They pointed at rocks, mountains, the sun, each other—each had a different signal group, confirming the agent's earlier assumption that they were not identical devices. But there also seemed to be a general term that took them all in.

He was not quite sure whether this term stood for machines in general, or could be taken as implying that the devices present were part of a single assembly, as he had suspected earlier. While the lessons went on, two of them wandered about the valley seeking new objects to show him. One of these objects proved the spark for a very productive line of thought.

Its shape, when it was brought back and shown to him, was as indescribable as that of many other things he had been shown by them. Its color was bright green and the agent, perceiving a rather wider frequency band than was usable by human eyes, did not see it or think of it as a green object. He narrowed its classification down to a much finer degree.

He did not know the chemical nature of chlorophyll, but

he had long since come to associate that particular reflection spectrum with photosynthesis. The thing did not seem to possess much rigidity. Its bulbous extensions sagged away from either side of the point where it was being supported. The handling extension that gripped it seemed to sink slightly into its substance.

He had never seen such a phenomenon elsewhere, and had no thought or symbol from the term *pulpy*. However, the concept itself rang a bell in his mind, for the machines facing him seemed fabricated from material of a rather similar texture. It was a peculiarity of their aspect that had been bothering him subconsciously ever since he had seen them moving. Now a nagging puzzlement—subconscious frustration was always unpleasant—was lifted from his mind.

The connection was not truly a logical one. Few new ideas have strictly logical connection with pre-existing knowledge. Imagination follows its own paths. Nevertheless, there was a connection, and, from the instant the thought occurred to him, the agent never doubted seriously that he was essentially correct. The natives of this planet did not merely use active carbon compounds as fuel for their machines. They constructed the machines themselves of the same sort of material!

Under the circumstances it was a reasonable thing to do— if one could succeed at it. The reactions of such chemicals were undoubtedly rapid enough to permit as speedy action as anyone could desire—at least as fast as careful thought could control. The agent's race had long since learned the dangers inherent in machines capable of responding to casual, fleeting thoughts and his ship's pickup-circuits were less sensitive, by far, than they might have been.

It was obvious why these devices were controlled from a distance, instead of being ridden by their operators, too. There must be some dangerous reactions, indeed, going on inside them. The agent decided it was just as well that his temporary prisoner had merely looked at the inside of his ship, without touching anything, and resolved to take no more such chances.

At any rate, there should be no more need for that sort of experiment. Language lessons were well under way. He had recorded a good collection of nouns, some verbs the machines had acted out, even an adjective or two. He was puzzled by the tremendous length of some of the signal groups, and suspected them of being descriptions, rather than individual basic words.

But even that theory had difficulties. The signal which, apparently, stood for the machines themselves, one which should logically have called for a rather long and detailed description, was actually one of the shortest—though even this took several hundred milliseconds to complete. The agent decided that there was no point in trying to deduce grammar rules. He could communicate with memorized symbols, and they would have to suffice.

Of course, the symbols that could be demonstrated on the spot were hardly adequate to explain the nature of Earth's danger. The Conservationist had long since decided just what he wished to say in that matter, and was waiting, impatiently, for enough words to let him say it.

It gradually became evident, however, that if he depended on chance alone to bring them into the lessons he was going to wait a long time. This meant little to him, personally. But the mole robots were not waiting for any instruction to be completed. They were burrowing on. The agent tried to think of some means for leading the lessons in the desired direction.

This took a good deal of imagination on his part, obvious as his final solution would seem to a human being. The idea of having to learn a language had been utterly strange to him, and he was still amazed at the ingenuity the natives showed, in devising a means for teaching one. It was some time before it occurred to him that *he* might very well perform some actions, just as *they* were doing. If he did *not* follow his own acts with signal groups of his own, these natives might not understand that he wanted theirs. The time had come for a more direct and audacious approach to the entire problem, and at the thought of what he was about to do his spirits soared.

He did it. He lifted the ship a few feet into the air, settled back to show that he was not actually leaving, and then rose again. He waited, expectantly.

"Fly."

"Up."

"Rise."

"Go.

Each of the watching machines emitted a different signal, virtually simultaneously. Three of them came through very faintly, since the speakers were some distance from the radio. But he was able to correlate each with the lip motions of its maker. He was not too much troubled by the fact that different signals were used. He was more interested in the evidence that a different individual was controlling each machine. This was a little confusing, in view of his earlier theories. But he stuck grimly to the problem at hand.

CHAPTER TWELVE

HAL AND CANDACE Parsons, and Truck MacLaurie were sitting on a relatively mud-less patch of earth, within comfortable watching distance of the alien. They had passed the saturation point in their general, rain-soaked misery, and the experience Truck had just been through had unnerved them all to the point where they desperately needed a rest.

Hal was putting Truck through something of a third degree. He was attempting to draw some specific information out of the athlete's unscholarly mind as to the precise nature of the alien's interior. It was proving to be rugged going, and his nerves were not in the best possible shape.

"Dammit!" he exploded, when Truck proved, for the twentieth time that he had no idea why he had been so suddenly allowed to leave. "The opportunity of the ages, and it has to be given a blockhead with an I.Q. of seventy-seven, who can't tell what it's all about!"

"Lay off him, honey," said Candace pointedly. "Truck's no blockhead. He's a blocking back, amongst other things. He just doesn't happen to be a scientist."

"Okay, if you say so." Hal ran unsteady fingers through his soaking-wet hair. "Sorry, Truck. It's just so infernally frustrating."

"Somebody's coming," said Truck with charitable forbearance, apparently unruffled by the catechism he had just been through. "Over there—look."

A muddy, heavily encumbered figure was approaching them through the rain and mist. Catching sight of them, it waved.

Truck, rising, advanced along the hillside to meet it, while Hal and Candace rose slowly to their feet. On closer approach, it proved to be a soldier, mud-soaked and carrying a movie camera slung over one shoulder, and what looked like a scintillometer over the other. Truck had quickly relieved the newcomer of a heavy walkie-talkie.

"Mr. and Mrs. Parsons?" the soldier said as he came up to them. "I'm General Wallace Eades. I've been talking to you upstairs long enough. I finally decided to make the drop myself."

"You don't know how glad we are to see you, General," said Candace, noting the two mud-dulled silver stars on the collar of his open shirt. "After three days with our friend over there..." she nodded toward the impassive, gray-metal globe, "...we were beginning to wonder if we were humans ourselves."

General Eades, his blue eyes unusually bright and young and alert in his lined, leathery face looked at the monstrous bulk of the alien and stood for a moment in silent speculation. Then he said, "I was beginning to think it was all a pipe-dream. He's a big fellow, isn't he?"

For the next few minutes, he talked with Hal, letting the geologist brief him on recent events. Then, turning to Truck, "Quite an experience for you, young man. If we get out of this thing in any sort of shape, you'll be in Hollywood in ten days."

"Coach wouldn't like it," said the football player. "And I'm no Elvis Presley."

General Eades put his head back and laughed. Then he unslung the movie camera and said, "I gather you haven't made a pictorial record of your friend over there. I don't know about you, but I don't want to be laughed out of the service. I thought you said he only had two eyes. Isn't that a third? Did you put mud in that one, too?"

"I'll be damned!" said Hal. He and Candace regarded one another. They were bewildered, amazed and a little frightened. His lips tightening, Hal said, "He's full of surprises. Stick around and you'll find out."

"I intend to," said General Eades. "I've been on this thing, ever since the first radar flash came in—four days ago. Haven't had two hours consecutive sleep since. You've got no idea the fuss our friend has kicked up. The army's got ten thousand men trying to crack this valley, and diplomats and newspaper men are sleeping on billiard tables in Butte—if they're lucky enough to buy space on one."

As he spoke, he walked slowly around the monstrous globe, holding the camera to eye level, shooting it from all sides. Returning, he reappropriated the walkie-talkie from Truck, who had been dutifully standing guard over it.

"I checked the stuff in your jeep and trailer on the way here from my drop," General Eades said. "You must have got more than just arm-tired cranking that battery outfit of yours. I haven't seen one like it since World War Two."

"It was the best the department at the University could allow us," said Hal, a trifle on the defensive.

Tactfully, Candace put in, "We're awfully glad you got here, General. We were not only wet—we were lonely for a new face."

"Afraid mine's not exactly new," said Eades. Then, putting the walkie-talkie to work, he said resignedly: "Guess I'd better report, before they send a big drop in, and a few-score G.I.'s get killed. This valley's full of rocks and potholes, and visibility is nil."

"You're telling us, General!" said Truck.

The general's report, via radio, was lengthy but concise. He had yet to complete it when an audition from the alien, mimicking his own voice, caused interference that made intelligible communication impossible. He lowered the set, looked at the others, and nodded toward the gray-metal globe.

"Is that it?" he asked.

"That's it," said Hal.

Almost before the words were out of his mouth, a new sound—not through the radio, but carried clearly through the open air—smote all their ears. Smote was the word, as it rose in an ear-shattering crescendo that caused them to look at one another in alarm.

"The thing's howling like a fire siren!" cried Candace, clapping her hands to her ears. The others followed suit.

It continued, for a couple of deafening minutes that all but reduced already quivering nerves to shreds. Then, as suddenly as it had started up, it ceased, and slowly they removed their hands.

Candace wondered if her eardrums were permanently damaged. She saw Truck hammering the side of his head, like an inexperienced swimmer with water in his ear.

He said, "If that's his natural voice, I wonder how he sounds when he's *really* worked up."

Hal and the general exchanged a significant look. It was Eades who broke the welcome silence. "Maybe he's right," he said. "Is that the first time it's tried communicating— apart from radio mimicry?"

"That's right," Hal told him.

"Significant," said General Eades. "Damned significant. I wonder... That third eye bothers me. Do you suppose it bothers him?"

He walked up to the machine, disregarding Candace's gasp, "Be careful!"

Gently he scraped the mud from the lens. Nothing happened, but the sound did not return. He said, scowling at the porthole, "The surface looks too flat for close vision."

"We had the same thought," Hal told him. "Still, it can see when it wants to."

General Eades walked around the sphere, studied the other two eyes, noted the places where the caked mud had flaked away. "Used to know an optometrist," he muttered.

"Could be, the mud helps to give him closer focus by covering most of the lens."

"...most of the lens," said the general, though his lips did not move. Eades started, looked at the others, and instantly pointed to one of his own eyes. He said, "Eye."

"Eye," said the voice from the alien. There was no question now in any of their minds. The alien had clearly discovered some means of direct vocal speech.

After several more tests, the general walked back to the others, his blue eyes alight with excitement. "That's it," he told them. "Our friend made that howl to let us know it had a new means of communication."

Hal motioned him to silence, and they waited, breathlessly. But the alien did not repeat the speech or any part of it. The geologist advanced, pointed to himself, and said, "Man."

"Man," said the alien.

"It understands," said Hal, his voice almost cracking. "Listen!" He accompanied the words by no pantomime, and the alien was silent.

"I'll be damned!" said the general.

"Eureka!" cried Candace, raising her arms toward the sky.

"Eureka!" said the voice from the globe.

"Careful, baby," Hal told her. "You just gave our friend a bum steer. Don't gesture unless you're outlining exactly what you mean."

From then on, in the excitement of attaining at least a rudimentary understanding with the thing from space, the little group on the hillside forgot the rain and their physical misery. Time was forgotten too, as they taught it new word meanings, and brought it examples of equipment and local flora in an effort to increase its vocabulary.

Candace found a bedraggled plant, wiped mud from it and said, "Green," pressing the stem as she held it up for the alien to see.

"Green," came the answer. "Plant—green."

"Green," Candace repeated. "Green through sun." She pointed skyward. "Green through photosynthesis."

"Plant green—through photosynthesis," came the expected reply. Then, "Plant, man green—both photosynthesis."

"Bless me!" cried General Eades. "We're on the way!"

Hal spoke up then. "Has it occurred to you, General, that our friend here may have some message to give us? If he has, it may take us a hell of a long time before we can give him the right words to give back to us."

Eades stroked his chin. "You were probably right in asking for philologists earlier," he said unhappily. "We're a bunch of babes in the woods at this game."

There was a long, disconsolate silence. Then Candace broke it, saying bravely, "In any case, we've got to keep going. Our friend may have an answer of his own."

"I'd give a lot for one good word—man I could count on getting down here alive," said the general. "I'll put in a call."

But, before he could get the radio to work, the observant Truck said, "Look! Hey, don't tell me he's leaving us now—"

They stared in horror and utter dismay as the great, gray bulk of the alien rose vertically in the roil of mud already familiar to all but the general. Then they breathed sighs of relief. It hovered, only a few feet above the ground, then settled back, then rose again and remained stationary.

"He's trying to signal to us!" cried Candace, her voice shrill with excitement. "He wants us to give him a word for what he's doing."

"Fly!" shouted the general.

"Up!" said Candace.

"Rise!" called Hal Parsons.

"Go!" yelled Truck MacLaurie.

They spoke almost simultaneously, but the monster from space seemed confused. He made no answer at all.

CHAPTER THIRTEEN

THE AGENT dropped back to the ground and went through his actions again. This time only the individual with the radio spoke. The word it used was Rise. This was not the one it had used the other time. To make sure, the agent went through the act still again, and got the same word. Evidently, once their minds were made up, they intended to stick to their decisions. What *could* he think?

Then he tried burrowing into the ground, which seemed a useful action to be able to mention. The word given on the radio was dig, though two of the other machines apparently had different ideas once more.

It did not occur to him that these things might be detecting the by-products of his digging as well as his deliberate attempts to produce sound waves, or that his efforts to focus his third eye lens, a little while before, had actually been the cause of their sudden interest in his ship at that moment. He was much too pleased with himself at this point to entertain such extraneous ideas.

Having taken over the initiative in the matter of language lessons, he concentrated on the words he wanted, and, within a fairly short time, felt sure that he could get the basic facts of Earth's danger across to his listeners. After all, only four signal groups were involved in the concept. Satisfied that he had these correctly, he proceeded to use them together. In his progress now he felt the surge of a very personal kind of pride.

"Man dig—mountain rise."

For some unexplained reason the listening machines did not burst into frantic activity at the news. For a moment, he hoped that the controllers had turned to more suitable equipment to cope with the danger, leaving inactive that which they had been using. But he was quickly disabused of that bit of wishful thinking. The machine with the radio began to speak again.

"Man dig." It bent over and began to push the loose dirt aside with the flattened ends of its upper struts.

The agent realized, with some dismay, that its operator must suppose he was merely continuing the language lesson. He spoke again, more loudly, the two signal groups that the other seemed to be ignoring.

"Mountain rise."

All the machines looked at the hill across the valley, but nothing constructive seemed likely to come from that. If they waited for that one to rise noticeably, it would be too late to do anything about enlightening them as to the robots. He tried, frantically, to think of other words he had learned, or combinations that would serve his purpose. One seemed promising to him.

"Mountain break—Earth break—man break." The verb did not quite fit what was to happen, according to its earlier demonstration, but it did carry an implication of destruction, at least. His audience turned back to the ship, but gave no obvious sign of understanding.

He thought of another concept that might apply, but no word for it had yet appeared in the lessons. So, to illustrate it, he turned his ship's weapon on a patch of soil, a hundred yards from the bow. Twenty seconds exposure to that needle of intolerable flame reduced the ground that it struck to smoking lava.

Even before he had finished, the word *fire* came from one of the watchers. The observer made no comment on the fact that the tube that threw slugs of metal had been leveled at his hull, during most of the performance. He simply made use of the new word.

"Man dig—Earth fire—mountain fire."

One of the machines produced its ionization tube and cautiously approached the patch of cooling slag. This had a slight amount of radioactivity from the beam, and its effect on the tube gave rise to much mutual signaling on the part of the machines. This culminated in a lengthy radio broadcast, not addressed to the agent. Then the language lessons were resumed, with the natives once more taking the initiative.

"Iron—copper—lead." Samples were shown individually.

"Metal." All the samples were shown together.

"Melt." This was demonstrated, when they finally made him understand that the weapon should be used again.

"Big—little." Pairs of stones, of cacti, coins and figures, scratched in the dirt, illustrated this contrast.

Numbers—no difficulty.

"Ship." This proved confusing, since the agent had supposed the word *man* covered any sort of machine.

Finally, slightly fuller sentences became possible.

"Fire-metal under ground," the men tried.

The agent repeated the statement, leaving them in doubt. More time passed, while *yes* and *no* were explained. Then the same phrase brought a response of "Yes."

"Men dig."

"Yes—men dig—mountain melt—mountain rise."

"Where?" This word took still more time, and was solved, at least, only by a pantomime involving all the men. *Here* and *there* were covered in the same act. However, knowing what the question meant did not make it much easier for the agent to answer it.

He had no maps of the planet, and would have recognized no man-made charts, with the possible exception of a globe, which is not standard equipment on a small field expedition.

After still more time, the men managed to get a unit of

distance across to him, however, and he could use the ion beam for pointing. In this way, he did his best to indicate the locations of the moles.

"There! Eighty-one miles. Two miles down." And, in another direction, "There! Fifteen hundred-twelve miles. Eighteen miles down." He kept this up through the entire list of the forty-five moles he had detected and located.

The furious note-taking that accompanied his exposition did not mean anything to him, of course, though he deduced correctly the purpose of the magnetic compass one of the listening machines was using. He realized that giving positions to an accuracy of one mile was woefully inadequate for the problem of actually locating the moles.

But he could do the final close-guiding later, when the native machines approached their targets. He could come to their aid if they did not have detection equipment of their own which would work at that range. Just what possibilities in that direction might be inherent in organic engineering the agent could not guess. At any rate, the natives did not seem to feel greater precision was needed. They made no request for it.

In fact, they did not seem to want anything more. He had expected to spend a long time explaining the apparatus needed to intercept and derange the moles. But that aspect of the matter did not appear to bother the natives at all. Why, why? It should have bothered them.

In spite of appearances, the agent was not stupid. The problem of communicating with an intelligence not of his own race had never, as far as he knew, been faced by any of his people. He had tried to treat it as a scientific problem. It was hardly his fault that each phenomenon he encountered had infinitely more possible explanations than ordinary scientific observation, and he could hardly be expected to guess the reason why.

Even so, he realized it could not be considered a proven fact that the natives had read the proper meaning from his signaling. He actually doubted that they had, in about the way and to about the extent that some mid-nineteenth century human physicists doubted the laws of gravity and conservation of energy. He determined to continue checking as long as possible, to make sure that they were right.

The human beings, partly as a result of greater experience, partly for certain purely human reasons, also felt that a check was desirable. With their far better local background, they were the first to take action. To them, *fire metal,* when mentioned in conjunction with a positive test for radioactivity, implied only one kind of fire.

Man dig was not quite so certain. They apparently could not decide whether the alien being was giving information or advice—whether someone was already digging at the indicated points, or that they should go there themselves to dig. The majority inclined to the latter view.

To settle the question, one of them took the trench-shovel, which was part of their equipment, and arranged a skit that eventually made clear the difference between the continuative—*digging*—and the imperative *dig!*

While this was going on, another thought occurred to the agent. Since these things had used different words for the machines he was watching and the one he was riding, perhaps *man* was not quite the right term for the mole-robots he was trying to tell about. He wondered how he could generalize. By the end of the second run-through of the skit he had what he hoped was a solution.

"Man digging—ship digging," he said.

"Digging fire metal?"

"Man digging fire metal—ship digging fire metal."

"Where?"

He ran through the list of locations again, though

somewhat at a loss for the reason it was needed, and was allowed to finish, because, though he did not know it, no one could think of a way to tell him to stop. He felt satisfied when he had finished—there could hardly be any doubt in the minds of his listeners now.

They were talking to each other again—the reason was now obvious enough. The operators must be in different locations, must be communicating with each other through their machines. He had little doubt of what they were saying, in a general way.

Which was too bad—in a general way.

"It's vague—infernally vague."

"I know—but what else can he mean?"

"Perhaps he's just telling about some of our own mines, asking what we get out of them or trying to tell us he wants some of it."

"But what can 'flame metal' mean but fissionables? And what mine of ours did he point out?"

"I don't know about all of his locations, but the first one he mentioned—the closest one—certainly fits."

"What?"

"Eighty-one miles, bearing thirty degrees magnetic. That's as close as you could ask to Anaconda, unless this map is haywire. There are certainly men digging there!"

"Not two miles down!"

"They will be, unless we find a substitute for copper."

"I still think this thing is telling us about beings of its own kind, who are lifting our fissionables. They could do it easily enough, if they dig the way this one does. I'm for at least calling up there, and finding out whether anyone has thought of drilling test cores under the mine level—and how deep they went. There's no point walking around here, looking for anything else. We've found our fireball, right here."

The agent was interested but not anxious when the machines turned back to him, and direct communication was brought once more into operation. He was feeling less tense, and he began to feel confident that everything was going to come out all right if he stuck with it.

"Eighty-one miles that way. Men digging. Go now."

They illustrated the last words, turning away from his ship and starting in the proper direction. The agent could not exactly relax, fitting as he did into the spaces designed for him in his ship, but he felt the appropriate emotion.

They were getting started on one of the necessary steps, at least. Presumably, the other and more distant ones would be tackled as soon as the news could be spread. These machines moved slowly, but their control impulses apparently did not.

It occurred to him that, since none of the devices had been left on hand to communicate with him, the natives might be expecting him to appear at the nearest digging site—the one they had mentioned. The more he thought of it, the more likely such an interpretation of their last message seemed. So, with the men barely started on their walk back to the waiting jeep, the Conservationist sent his ship whistling upward on a long slant toward the northeast.

CHAPTER FOURTEEN

THAT THE multiple answer had puzzled the star-traveler became evident when he dropped back to the ground and went through the entire process a second time. This time, General Eades took over, employing Hal Parsons' definition… "Rise."

Apparently, the switch in words from one member of the party to another troubled the alien, for he dropped gently. Then he rose and hung in the air once more, a few feet above the muddy soil. The general repeated, "Rise," and after a few seconds of motionless hovering the alien dropped back to the ground and did not go through the performance a fourth time.

"I wish our experimental boys would come up with an anti-grav like that," said the general, in a wistful aside. "It would sure give us the jump on you-know-who. Wonder where he gets all that power from."

"You and me both," murmured Truck MacLaurie. "What a bucking-machine he'd make for practice."

Candace giggled, and Hal looked at her, then despairingly at Truck. To give him solace, Candace said, "Just think, honey, the progress we've made in the last few hours. Only a little while back, we were nowhere."

"I wish I felt it was getting us anywhere," said the unhappy geologist. "When we started out looking for minerals, I never figured we'd come up against anything like this."

The general motioned them to silence, saying, "He's up to something new. Lordy! Just look at him dig!"

Candace said, "He's burrowing…that's all. What did you expect?"

Truck cried, "He's mining!"

"Will you shut up," said Hal rudely, as General Eades scowled unhappily at the confusion-potential of another multiple answer. Another howling siren rose from the alien. But it was neither as enduring nor as ear shattering as his earlier signal.

"Sorry, honey," Candace whispered when it was over.

It became quickly evident that the leadership in the language lesson had been reversed. Evidently having decided he had learned all he could from human demonstration, the visitor was demonstrating on his own, hoping the humans could supply the definitions he sought.

"I'd give my stars to know what he's trying to get through," said the general softly. "It must be important, if he's come all the way from God knows what star to give it to us."

There was another growl from the alien, which all four of them took as a request for silence. From then on, the reverse lesson went on apace. The only difficulty was that the words evidently sought by the visitor made little sense to his watchers.

"Man dig—mountain rise," came the message.

They stared at one another, uncomprehending. Finally, with a shrug, the general bent over awkwardly, hampered as he was by the walkie-talkie, and began scraping a hole in the mud with his fingers.

"Man dig," Eades said, as he did so.

"Mountain rise."

There was insistence in the aliens words, which caused all four of his listeners to turn toward the ragged range-crests, which was barely visible now through the rain and mist on the far side of the valley. There was further confusion, when the great, gray globe gave voice to the strange words, "Mountain break—Earth break—man break."

Then, came sudden, unexpected, frightening demonstration in action. For the second time since its discovery an opening appeared in the dully gleaming, curved surface of the alien—an opening both smaller and more menacing than the one that had all but led Truck to his doom.

A snout appeared, swiveled past the watching group, and from it there emerged a darting, blinding ray of light—or heat. It struck the muddy hillside a hundred yards or so away and with frightful, eruptive violence a patch of the soggy soil itself began to bubble and turn, first red, then white-hot. A trickle of fluid, molten material ran slowly down the hillside, and a cloud of white steam rose high in the air. Once more, the sense of intolerable heat was present.

"My God!" exclaimed a white-lipped Hal Parsons. "He's set fire to the earth itself!" He picked up the rifle, which he was still carrying, unslung its cover and aimed it at the hull-opening, pushing Candace behind him as he did so.

"Put that toy away, Parsons," said the general with grim insistence. "It won't do a damned bit of good. Do you understand? Put it away."

The intolerable ray of heat vanished, and the opening in the alien's hull disappeared as abruptly as it had opened. The visitor said, slowly, "Man dig—Earth fire—mountain fire."

"Let's have the scintillometer," the general said to Truck. "It's a lot better than that Geiger job you've been using."

"I can work it," said Hal. Taking the instrument, and adjusting it, he walked over to the rapidly cooling, but still semi-molten spot that the heat-ray had turned to lava. The count ran high and fast as he approached it. Turning back to the general, he said, "No doubt about it—she's plenty hot."

"Got to report this," said Eades tersely. "He's trying to get something through, all right—and I don't like the looks of it. Maybe some of those eggheads sitting around in Butte can give us a clue."

It was a lengthy broadcast, relayed through the radio of a helicopter hovering above the clouds. When it was over, the general signed off in disgust.

"How do you like that?" he said, to no one in particular. "Those broad-beamed boffins want us to carry on." He cursed, fluently, effectively, and then added, "Sorry, ma'am," to Candace without turning a gray hair.

She said, "Maybe we'd better try him on minerals alone."

So, the lesson continued, until some of the confusion about various stones and metals, upon the nature of machines, was partially cleared up. Then came the alarming statement, "Yes—men dig—mountain melt—mountain rise."

"Is he trying to tell us *men* are planting volcanoes under us?" Candace asked incredulously.

"He's trying to tell us someone or something is," her husband told her grimly. "Ask him where, General?"

This led to laborious exchanges, establishing direction and distance units, after which the alien began issuing his information, as to the location of the horrors to come if his warnings were ignored. While this was going on, Parsons took notes, doing his best to write legibly on limp paper. Finally Candace, who had once learned shorthand, took over the job.

General Eades turned toward her and said, "That seems to be all. Got them?"

"All forty-five, General," said Candace. "Want me to read them back to you?"

"Not yet," said Eades. "I want to know what he means by *men* digging volcanoes."

The results weren't satisfactory, and so the alien went through the list again. Then, in desperation, the general got into touch with the higher-ups once more. He talked long and determinedly and with authority. He concluded with, "...There's absolutely no point in walking around here, looking for anything else. We've found our fireball, right here."

He paused, looked at the impassive facade of the alien inquiringly. "More?" he asked. "Anything more?"

The voice, so oddly human, so utterly like his own in tone

and inflection, replied, "Eighty-one miles that way. Men digging. Go now."

"Okay," said the general. "That's the message." And, to the alien, "Eighty-one miles that way. Men digging. Go now." He motioned to the others to follow, and led the way through the rain toward the jeep.

"You're not going to leave him?" Candace asked, incredulously.

"It may take all of us to get out of this damned valley," Eades told her. "If what he reported is true—no matter how garbled—our work is at Anaconda. That's where the nearest trouble is, according to him. We'll have weasels in here by tomorrow, to do a proper survey job. Complete with scients..." Then, with a look of apology, "Sorry, folks, I mean specialists. You've done great."

"That's okay, General," said Truck, in his easy-going drawl.

The others laughed.

Candace said, "This probably sounds screwy, but I'm going to miss our globular friend. He was—"

"Not *he—it,*" said Parsons. "Why must you give it sex?"

"Forget about sex," the general told them, masking a smile. "We're going to have one sweet job getting out of here."

Candace looked back, through the mist and rain and darkness of approaching twilight, and suddenly uttered a cry of alarm. "Look!" she said, grabbing the nearest arm, which happened to belong to the general. "He's taking off!"

They watched, all with mixed emotions, as the alien rose vertically from its hillside bed, and hovered a moment at mountaintop level. Then it suddenly veered, moved swiftly toward the north and disappeared.

"Well," said Truck. "Goodbye."

And that seemed to sum it up. Before they had the jeep halfway up the pass the rain had stopped, and there was a break of afterglow gold in the western sky.

CHAPTER FIFTEEN

THE MOMENT HE rose above the valley, the Conservationist picked up the radar beams again—the beams that had startled him when he first approached the strange planet. As had happened on the earlier occasion, a few milliseconds served to bring many more of them to bear upon him.

He was quite evidently being watched on this journey. But he no longer expected these beams to carry intelligent speech. More or less casually, he noted their points of origin. He wondered, for brief moments, whether it might not be worth while to investigate them later, but felt fairly certain that it wouldn't. He turned his full attention on his goal.

The crusts of clay had fallen from his eyes as he flew, and he was once again limited to long-distance vision. He could make out the vast, terraced pits of the great copper mine as he approached, but could not distinguish the precise nature of the moving objects within. He did not consider sight a particularly useful or convenient sense anyway, so he settled to the ground, half a mile from the pit's edge, bored in as he had before, and began probing with seismic detectors and electrical senses.

He had, of course, already known of the presence of the hole. A fair amount of seismic activity had reached his original landing spot from this place, enabling him to deduce its shape fairly accurately. Now, however, he realized—and for the first time—the amount of actual work going on. There were many machines of the sort he had already seen, which was hardly surprising. But there were many others as well, and the fact that most of them were metallic in construction startled him considerably.

There was a good deal of electrical activity, and at first he had hopes of finding an actual native. But these hopes quickly faded when he discovered there was nothing at all suggestive of thought-patterns. Some of the machines were magnetically driven. Others used regular electrical impulses for, apparently, starting the chemical reactions that furnished their main supply of energy.

The really surprising fact was the depth of the pit. If this work had begun since the receipt of his information, the wretched, guilty robots would be caught without difficulty. It took some time, by his perception standards, for a truer picture of the situation to be forced on his mind.

The pit had not been started recently. The progress of the diggers was fantastically slow. Clumsy metal scoops raised a few tons of material at a time and deposited it in mobile containers that bore it swiftly away. Fragments of the pit-wall were periodically knocked loose by expanding clouds of ionized gas, apparently formed chemically. The shocks initiated by these clouds were apparently the origin of most of the temblors he had felt from this source, while he was still eighty miles away.

His electrical analysis finally gave him the startling, incredible facts. This was a copper mine—extracting ore far poorer in quality than any his own people could afford to process. This race was certainly confined, for some reason, to its home planet, and had been driven to picking leaner and ever leaner ores to maintain its civilization.

The development of organic machines had given them a reprieve from barbarism and final extinction, but surely could not save them forever. Why in the galaxy, did they not use the organic robots for digging directly, as he had seen them do, during the language lessons? One would think that metal would be far too precious to such planet-bound people, for them to waste even iron on bulky, clumsy devices such as those at work here!

Even granting that the machines he had originally seen, and which seemed the most numerous, were not ideally designed for excavation work, surely, surely, better ones could be made. A race that could do what this race had done with carbon compounds could have no lack of ingenuity—or, more properly, of creative genius.

Very slowly, he realized why they had not—and why his mission was futile. He realized why these people would be doomed, even if the moles had never been planted. He noticed something relevant, during the conversation, but had missed its full staggering implication. The organic compounds were soft. They bent and sagged and yielded to every sort of external mechanical influence—it was a wonder, thinking about it, that the machines he had seen held their shapes so well. No doubt, there was a framework of some sort, perhaps partly metallic even though he had not perceived it.

But such things could never force their way through rock. The only way they *could* dig was with the aid of metallic auxiliaries—simple ones, such as those used to illustrate the verb to him, or more capacious and complex ones like those in use here.

This race was doomed, had been doomed long before the poachers ever approached their planet. They needed metal, as any civilization did. They were bound to their world, but kept from moving about even upon it, for not one in a thousand of these people could conceivably travel by machine, as the agent's race did. The organic engines could not possibly be used as vehicles. They could not be so used because their very essential nature of chemical violence made them untouchable.

These people were trapped in a vicious circle, using their

metal to dig more metal, sparing what little they could for electrical machinery and other equipment needed to a society, always having less and less to spare, always using more and more to get it. The idea that they could survive, until the planet's natural processes renewed the supply, was ridiculous.

It was, in short, precisely the same tragic circle that the agent's own race was precariously avoiding, millennium after millennium, by its complex schedule of freighters that distributed the metal from each planet in turn among thousands of others, then either waited for nature to renew the supply, or "tickled up" uninhabitable worlds as the poachers had done to this one.

Metal kept the machines operating. The machines kept food flowing to that vast majority of individuals who could not travel in search of it. A single break in the transport schedule could starve a dozen worlds. It was a fragile system, at best, and no member of the race liked to think about— much less actually face—examples of its failure.

The agent's mounting discomfort as he considered the matter of Earth was natural and inevitable. This race was what his own might have been, hundreds of millions of years before, had means of space-travel not been developed. They would probably be extinct before the poachers' torpedoes began to take effect, which was, no doubt, a mercy.

The agent could not help them. Even if the communication problem were cracked, they could not be brought into the transport network of civilization for untold millennia. No, they were truly lost—a race under sentence of extinction. The reorganization necessary was frightening in its complexity, even to him. Teaching them to build and use the equipment of his ship would be utterly useless, since it was entirely metallic, and they would be even worse off than with their organic devices.

They were already, probably by chemical means, stripping

ores more efficiently than his own people, so he could hardly help them there. No, it was a virtual certainty that, when the planet's crust began to heave as giant bathyliths built up beneath it, when rivers of lava poured from vents scattered over the planet, no one would be there to face it.

This was a relief, in a way. The agent could picture, all too vividly, the plight of seeing a close friend engulfed only a few miles away, and having to spend hours or years of uncertainty, wondering when his own area would be taken— and then knowing.

That was the worst. There was plenty of warning, as far as awareness was concerned. Anywhere from minutes to years and millennia, if one was a really good computer. You knew, and if you had a mobile machine, you could move out of the way. Even these organic machines traveled fast enough for that. But only machines would let a being get out of the way—and there would be no machines here by then.

He wished with every atom of his being that he had never detected the poachers, had never seen this unfortunate planet or heard of its race. No good had come of it—or very little, anyway. There would, admittedly, be metal here before long, brought up with the magma flows, borne by subcrustal convection-currents in the stress-fluid that formed most of the worlds bulk.

The poachers would be coming back for it, and he could at least deprive them of that. He would beam a report in toward the heart of the galaxy, making sure it did not radiate in the direction they had taken. Then there would be freighters to forestall them.

It was ironic, in a way. If any of this race should have survived the disturbance that would bring back the metal, that disturbance would be the salvation both of their species and their civilization. Most probably, however, the only witnesses would be a few half-starved, dull-minded barbarians, who would wonder, dimly, what was happening for a little while before temblors shattered their bodies forever.

There was nothing to keep him here, and the place was distasteful. More of the organic robots were approaching his position, but he did not want to talk any more. He wanted to forget this planet, to blot the memory of it forever from his mind.

With abrupt determination, he sent the dirt boiling away from his hull in a rising cloud of dust, pointed his vessel's blunt nose into the zenith and applied the drive. He held back just enough to keep his hull temperature within safe limits, while he was still in the atmosphere.

Then, with detectors fanning out ahead, he swung back to the line of his patrol orbit, and began accelerating away from the Solar system. Ignorant of events behind him, he never sensed the flight of swept-winged metal machines that hurtled close below while he was still in the air, split seconds after he had left the ground.

He did not notice the extra radar beam that fastened itself on his hull, while the machine projecting it flung itself through the sky, computing an interception course. This was too bad, for the relays in that machine would have made him feel quite at home, and its propulsion mechanism would have given him more food for thought.

He might have sensed its detonation, for his pursuer had a nuclear warhead. But its built-in brain realized, as quickly as the agent himself could have, that no interception was possible within its performance limits. It gave up, shutting off its fuel and curving back toward its launching station. Even the aluminum alloys in its hull would have interested the agent greatly—but he was trying to think of anything except Earth, its inhabitants and their appalling technology.

His patrol orbit would carry him back to this vicinity in

half a million years or so. The freighters would have been there by that time.

He wondered if he could bring himself to look at the dead world.

IT WAS THE general who explained it to the Parsons, at the University a few weeks later. He said, "He must have been in the devil's own hurry. All he did was get his warning through, take a quick look at Anaconda, and zoom off. Ground-to-Air sent up a nuclear rocket to intercept him, but he got clear of it just in time, thank God! Plenty of heads rolled after that foul-up, I can assure you. Trigger-happy idiots they were."

Candace, looking exceptionally attractive in a new, soft-blue linen dress which almost miraculously complemented both her figure and her coloring, said, "I'm glad, too. It must have had something to do with his intuitive alertness, from what I've been able to gather. Perhaps, he thought this world was going to blow up at any minute."

"Hah!" said General Eades. "We've already located nine of those damned underground borers he told us about. At the rate they're moving, our fiftieth-generation descendants will be out in space themselves before anything catastrophic happens. We'll have the whole bunch spotted and disarmed by that time."

He paused, chuckled again and added, "The weird part of it is that twenty-seven of the damned monsters are doing their stuff under Iron Curtain soil."

Hal Parsons spoke thoughtfully. "I've been reading some of the pull-together reactions in the headlines, General. Won't all this put you out of a job?"

"Not for a while," said Eades. "Actually, I hope so. No responsible soldier wants war—ever. Makes our uniforms too dusty."

"I still wish I knew how he produced that rain," said Candace. "I've added meteorology to my other duties, hoping to get to the bottom of it."

"Probably, he was just taking a bath," said Eades. He puffed on his cigar meditatively and added, "It's good to know you got a full professorship out of it, Parsons—and that you're on your way to one yourself, Mrs. Parsons." He fingered the new, bright extra star on his own collar, then asked, "What happened to the big, good-looking kid you had with you? I thought for sure he'd be in Hollywood by now."

"Oh—poor Truck," replied Candace. "He was all set to go. But he wanted to play in the homecoming game first. He broke his nose, and right now the movie brass isn't interested. But he doesn't seem to mind. He's making out fine with one of those cute little red-headed co-eds on the campus."

"I'm glad to hear it," said the general. He paused, frowning. "You know, it's funny—but ever since that damned metal monster flew out of our lives, I feel as if I'd lost a friend."

"I feel the same way," said Hal.

"I guess we all do," said Candace. She was much too wise, being a woman, to add, "I told you so."

THE END